Shattering Hamlet's Mirror

Shattering
Hamlet's Mirror

THEATRE AND REALITY

Marvin Carlson

ANN ARBOR
UNIVERSITY OF MICHIGAN PRESS

First paperback edition 2018
Copyright © by Marvin Carlson 2016
All rights reserved

Published in the United States of America by the
University of Michigan Press
Manufactured in the United States of America
♾ Printed on acid-free paper

2021   2020   2019   2018   5   4   3   2

A CIP catalog record for this book is available from the British Library.

Library of Congress Cataloging-in-Publication Data

Names: Carlson, Marvin, 1935– author.
Title: Shattering Hamlet's mirror : theatre and reality / Marvin Carlson.
Description: Ann Arbor : University of Michigan Press, 2016. | Includes
     bibliographical references and index.
Identifiers: LCCN 2015046847| ISBN 9780472119851 (hardback) | ISBN
     9780472121861 (e-book)
Subjects: LCSH: Theater—Philosophy. | BISAC: PERFORMING ARTS /
     Theater / General. | PERFORMING ARTS / Theater / History &
     Criticism.
Classification: LCC PN2039 .C255 2016 | DDC 792.01—dc23
LC record available at http://lccn.loc.gov/2015046847

ISBN 978-0-472-03724-7 (paper)

For Bert States
who was fascinated by both Crab and Hamlet

. . . the purpose of playing, whose end, both at the first and now, was and is, to hold, as 'twere, the mirror up to nature . . .

 —Hamlet in *Hamlet*

I love acting; it is so much more real than life.

 —Henry in *The Portrait of Dorian Grey*

Pretense! Reality! To hell with it all!

 —The Stage Manager in *Six Characters in Search of an Author*

Contents

Introduction

The Imitation of What?

Any consideration of the relationship between the theatre, at least in the Western world and the real world, must almost inevitably begin with a discussion of the term *mimesis*. There is surely no other critical term that holds so central a position in Western critical discourse involving the theatre and drama, and none so directly involved with the manner in which the theatre relates to the real world in which it is embedded. Mimesis was a key term for both of the founding fathers of that discourse, Plato and Aristotle, and the subject of countless theoretical essays ever since, with the inevitable result that the term has been employed in the support of a very wide range indeed of analytic projects and thus acquired an enormous range of associations and implications. Ever since the ancient Greeks, though, there has been a general agreement that a central characteristic of theatre as an art and indeed as a human activity is that it imitates, and in their discussion of the dynamics of this imitation, Plato and Aristotle employed the term mimesis.

To raise the apparently simple question of what in fact theatre imitates is, however, to enter into a realm of considerable confusion and disagreement. Perhaps there would be the broadest consensus on the idea that theatre imitates life, but then, of course, one must confront the question of what the "life" is that theatre is imitating. Again, the most likely response to this question would probably be something like "observed reality," and for an important part of theatre history, often referred to as the period of realism, that response would have seemed adequate. Yet if one looks at the full range of theatre, it is clear that realism has been only a particular style of dramatic production, and by no means always the dominant one. "Observed reality" was clearly not what the Greek dramatists, or for that matter the Elizabethans, the French neoclassicists, or the contributors to the various modern "isms" were seeking. What they sought to imitate in fact was a reality behind observed reality, a concept already central to Plato and Aristotle, whose works provide the grounding of the Western tradition of what mimesis is.

To begin at the beginning, then, although Plato and Aristotle disagreed about the exact nature of what mimesis was imitating, they did agree that it was not any physical object actually in the world but an abstraction from an ideal realm of which our own world was a less fully realized reflection. For Plato, this abstraction was static, an idea in the mind of God. Aristotle did not reject the concept of such a static realm but saw the world as in process, striving toward such an ideal but perhaps never achieving it. Aristotle's concept of imitation was not only more positive but more dynamic, since what was being imitated was not particular objects, but a process. In the *Physics*, Aristotle observes that "art in a sense completes what nature is unable to finish, and in a sense imitates nature."[1]

Plato, postulating a static realm of ideas in the mind of God, saw imitation as a reflection of this static world, but according to his thought, imitation was of two kinds—one natural and in harmony with the operations of the world—the other artificial and a source of illusion to be condemned. This distinction is clearly laid out in the famous passage that opens the tenth book of *The Republic*, about the three kinds of beds. Plato presents three kinds of creators: God, the carpenter, and the painter. From the mind of God comes the single unique idea of an object—in this case, a bed. The carpenter who creates a physical copy of this idea is a proper imitator, working, like nature, to create copies of the divine idea. The painter, however, imitates not the divine idea but the physical copy in the world, and thus creates an inferior imitation. His creations are not true imitations but only appearances, imitations of other imitations.[2] In a related passage, Plato applies to this process another image, which, rephrased by Shakespeare in the words of Hamlet, becomes one of the most famous statements concerning imitation in the Western tradition. Says Socrates: "If you're prepared to take a mirror and turn it round everywhere, you'll soon produce the sun and the objects in the sky, soon produce the earth, soon produce yourself and other creatures and objects and plants, and everything that was mentioned a moment ago." To this Glaucon replies, with Socrates's approval: "Yes, their appearance, but surely not their genuine actuality."[3] Clearly this anticipates Hamlet's "mirror held up to nature," though seen as a negative and misleading process by Plato, an example of false imitation.

The Greek concept of the object of imitation as idealized reality was taken up as central to the neoclassic theatre, with its identification of "la belle Nature" as the object of imitation not only in the theatre, but in the arts in general. In the *Encyclopedia*, that compendium of Enlightenment knowledge, the Chevalier Louis de Jaucourt begins the entry on "la belle Nature" by defining it as "nature embellished, perfected by the fine arts for use and entertainment." He traces this concept back to Plato and Aristotle, who broke away, he argues, from the earlier art forms of the barbarian past, which utilized imitation, but a "gross imitation, of gross nature itself. All art consisted of presenting whatever one saw or heard. Selection was unknown." It was the Greeks who discovered that "it was not enough to imitate things" but that one must reveal their hidden beauty by selection and arrangement. He distinguishes between two "modes of imitation": that of the portrait-painter, who merely copies observed reality, and that the Greeks chose, which was to seek "general beauty."[4] Certainly Plato agreed with the inferiority of the painter as a portrayer of observed reality, but neoclassicism by no means condemned painting in general, as Plato did, but only painting that presented unadorned nature and not the ideal behind it.

In fact this is clearly not what Plato had in mind, but the neoclassic understanding of Plato on this subject as filtered through the interpretation of the late classic Neoplatonists, and especially Plotinus, who provided a critical corrective to Plato's suspicion of the arts. Plotinus agreed with Plato that a purer idea of beauty lay beneath the observed world, but felt that art could in fact access it directly through mimesis. In a key passage of his *Enneads*, he argues that the arts "give no bare reproduction of the thing seen but go back to the Reason-Principle from which Nature itself derives," and further that "they are holders of beauty and add where nature is lacking."[5] Clearly the first of these points uses Plato's argument to defend art's access to the ideal through mimesis, while the second draws upon the more teleological view of Aristotle of art as completing observed nature.

Although Aristotle's *Poetics* is a foundational text for dramatic theory, neither he nor Plato, in speaking of mimesis in art, is really talking about how mimesis operates in the art of the performed theatre. Aristotle focuses upon the dynamics of the dramatic text, and his imitation of an action is essentially a literary matter, not a physical one. Plato also looks primarily to literature, especially Homer, even though he does evoke painting in his example of the bed.

An important strand of Western writing on mimesis follows this literary orientation, most famously in what is generally considered the classic work in the field, Erich Auerbach's monumental 1946 study, *Mimesis: The Representation of Reality in Western Literature.*

This important aspect of mimetic study leads us away, however, from its implications for the art of theatre, and again we can return to Plato and Aristotle for a clarification of this point. In fact, the more the study of the representation of reality moves toward literary narration, the more it approaches what Plato calls *diegesis,* an alternative to mimesis, in that the former imparts information by telling and the latter by showing.

Aristotle devotes very little attention to the nontextual aspects of theatre. He notes that epic poetry, tragedy, and comedy and the poetic dithyramb are all modes of imitation, differing in medium, objects, and the manner or mode of imitation. Only in the third does Aristotle address what more recent authors would doubtless consider the central distinguishing characteristic of theatre, that in it the poet does not speak in his own person, in the manner of Homer, but "presents all his characters as living and moving before us."[6] There is no further development of any of the implications of using living material, which presumably would be a part of spectacle, one of the Aristotle's six parts of drama, and for Aristotle the least important and least artistic. Indeed, he notes in his extremely brief comments on this subject that we may be sure that the power of tragedy "is felt even apart from representation and actors."[7]

Upon physical presentation, Plato has even less to say. His key example of the mimetic artist is the painter, although unquestionably he would see the dramatist in the same way as an imitator of imitations, here of human beings, like the portrait-painter dismissed by Jaucourt. From a more modern perspective we might ask the troubling question of what would be the status of the actual bed created by the Plato's carpenter, according to him a legitimate form of mimesis, if it were then utilized in a theatrical production. It would surely not then be an imitation of an imitation, like the painting of the bed, because it would remain in fact the same physical bed. The question of what happens to mimesis in such a situation, standing outside the systems established by Plato and Aristotle, leads us to the central question of this book: what challenges to representation and to mimesis arise from the fact that the dramatic artist, unlike the painter, utilizes material from the real world to create his art?

Within the tradition of Western literature and performance, this sort of question did not arise in any serious form until fairly recently, really not until the twentieth century. Of course Plato and Aristotle were well aware that a distinctive feature of the drama was its utilization of observed objects. This is precisely the point made by Plato in Book III of *The Republic* when he distinguishes between two basic ways of presenting events, by narration, or telling (diegesis), and by imitation or showing (mimesis). In classical times, what was primarily shown was the costumed and masked bodies of actors. In the Renaissance, increasingly elaborate backgrounds were created for these bodies, but these backgrounds functioned visually in much the same way as conventional paintings, and indeed scenery that was essentially flat paintings, even when these were made up of multiple pieces, remained the theatre's standard visual accompaniment to the actor until the romantic era. Even objects like tables, dressers, and chairs were still often painted onto flat backgrounds at many theatres well into the nineteenth century. Under these circumstances, the only objects onstage that also had an independent existence in the world outside the theatre were the actors, and theorists of the theatre, primarily concerned, like Aristotle, with the dramatic text, did not find this double existence of any particular interest or significance.

The first serious interest in actors as inhabitants of both a real and a fictive world appeared in the eighteenth century with the development of an interest in the analysis and understanding of the art of acting itself. This interest was not yet concerned with the particular situation of the actor as a body inhabiting two worlds, but rather with exploring a fresh perspective on the dynamics of mimesis. From almost the beginning of critical writing on acting, in mid-eighteenth-century France, the subject inspired two distinctly opposed schools of thought. On the one hand there was the position first clearly articulated by Luigi Riccoboni in 1738, that for an actor to create an effective stage illusion, he must capture the "tones of the soul," too varied and complex to be learned mechanically, but only by tapping into his own personal emotions.[8] This position was first challenged as early as 1750 by Riccoboni's own son, Antonio, who argued that on the contrary, such emotional involvement would work against effective acting and that the best actor would observe and closely imitate the natural reactions of others by technical control of himself.[9] This position would of course be most famously articulated by Diderot in his classic *Paradox on the Actor*.

Both positions are closely tied to important shifts taking place in the social and cultural world of eighteenth-century Europe, and both provide important insights into how thinking about the mimetic process was changing during this century. What the actor championed by the elder Riccoboni is imitating is the movements of his own soul, which provides a truth more fundamental than the observed reality advanced as the model for imitation by his son. One can detect distinct echoes of classic theory, especially of Plato—or, more accurately, of Plotinus here—although the idea in the mind of God has been replaced by insight into the deepest workings of nature. Clearly we are moving toward a romantic attitude here, and of course Rousseau, one of the central figures in the creation of European romanticism, was deeply influenced by Plato and deeply suspicious of theatre, for much the same reason—that it imitated not the deep truths of nature, but the passing fads and fancies of everyday life. As romantic theory and romantic drama developed, this view would reinforce the concept of the romantic dramatist and the romantic actor as inspired geniuses, whose work imitated not surface reality, but the visions into the heart of nature gained by these geniuses within their own sensitive psyches.

The opposing intellectual position of Diderot and the younger Riccoboni, however, drew upon other and equally influential intellectual trends of the century, particularly empiricism and the increasing focus upon scientific rationalism. These encouraged a view of human understanding that was not based upon internal inspiration or abstract Platonic or Neoplatonic ideas but upon the presumably objective observations of sensory experience. In the theatre this view was closely allied to that of the new bourgeois public that was replacing the aristocratic audiences of the previous era. They favored theatre that reflected their own observed reality—characters, situations, and surroundings that imitated their experienced world. This interest was answered by a new mode of drama developed and theorized during this century by George Lillo, Gotthold Lessing, Denis Diderot, and others, which evolved into the modern realistic drama most notably associated with the middle period of Henrik Ibsen and the work of his countless imitators.

Clearly the object of imitation within this tradition, which dominated the Western theatre during most of the nineteenth and twentieth centuries, was the observed world. The highest praise for an actor in this theatrical tradition was that he or she did not appear to be acting, but to be "living" the role, presenting a character indistinguishable from someone encountered in real life. Conversely, an actor who did not give a convincing imitation of "real life" might well be condemned for being artificial, mannered—in short, too "theatrical." It is important to remember, however, that from the younger Riccoboni and Diderot onward, the critical and theoretical assumption was that this effect was achieved by technical skill. It was still fundamentally a mimetic process. The best actor was one who carefully observed and impeccably imitated reality. An excellent early example of this concept was David Garrick, whose work was central in establishing a new fascination with realism in the European theatre. Garrick's early biographer, Arthur Murphy, recounts a story from the very beginning of Garrick's career, in the early 1740s, when he enjoyed one of his first great triumphs in *King Lear*. Garrick reports that he found a way to portray Lear's madness by observing a friend in an asylum who had lost his reason after accidentally dropping his baby daughter to her death. Observing the distraught father's obsessive reenactment of that event, Garrick reported, was how "*I learned to imitate madness*; I copied nature, and to that owed my success in *King Lear*."[10]

Garrick's more realistic style of acting was a revelation and model to leading players of the late eighteenth century, especially in England and France, and under his direction Drury Lane became one of the leading theatres of Europe. There, Garrick extended his interest in realism beyond acting to the whole apparatus of production, including scenery, lighting, and costumes. Critical to his reforms in these scenic concerns was his employment of Philippe-Jacques de Loutherbourg, who joined him in 1771. Traditionally, European scenic designers had their backgrounds in architecture, producing monumental but rather sterile and neutral collections of columns, stairways, halls, and arches, generally painted on flat backgrounds. De Loutherbourg was, on the contrary, a landscape painter, who brought a new interest in physical nature, atmosphere, and even the representation of actual places to stage scenery.

All of the visual concerns of de Loutherbourg corresponded very well to the literary concerns of romanticism in the theatre, the early variations of which were appearing in England and Germany at just this time—the interest in physical nature, in atmosphere, in the kind of specificity that was later called "local color," all were central to the romantic imagination, and as romantic scene design developed during the next generation across Europe, it very much followed the patterns de Loutherbourg had established at Drury Lane.

What this meant visually was that scenery, like acting, began to imitate observed nature, often in striking or extreme forms. Many of the great romantic actors followed Garrick's imitation of real madness by similar extreme emotional displays, and when the leading Italian romantic scene designer Alessandro Sanquirico traveled to Vesuvius to gain the model for an erupting volcano at La Scala in Milan in 1827, scenic designers all over Europe followed his example. Coincidentally, this same year, which saw one of the most famous of the romantic scenic designs in Italy, saw in France the publication of the most famous manifesto of the romantic drama, Victor Hugo's *Preface to Cromwell*. At one point in that essay, Hugo directly addresses the question of theatrical scenery, dismissing as improbable and absurd the banal neutral vestibules and antechambers of traditional tragedy instead of "exact localization," which is demanded by the present time with its insistence upon the presentation of reality. Would the poet, Hugo asks rhetorically," dare to assassinate Rizzio anywhere but in Mary Stuart's chamber?" or "burn Joan of Arc anywhere but in the Old Market?" "Nature then!" He concludes, "Nature and truth" must be what the modern theatre must make the basis of its imitation.

This is certainly not "la belle Nature" of the eighteenth century, which Hugo dismisses as an attempt to "correct nature," but it is also distinctly not the unadorned nature that would, at least in theory, mark the work of the later so-called naturalists. "Truth in art" Hugo insists, "could never be considered *absolute* reality, as several writers have claimed. Art cannot produce the thing itself." He continues with a reductio ad absurdum by way of applying this argument to Corneille's *The Cid*. First, his imaginary critic complains that the Cid is speaking in verse, then that he is speaking French, not Spanish, and finally questions why we do not see the real Cid, in flesh and blood, instead of some actor named Pierre or Jacques? Once one gives in to this logic, Hugo warns, there is no end. One would have to demand "next that the sun replace the footlights and *real* trees and houses replace those deceitful sets."[11] Ironically, of course, the modern theatre has seen the fulfillment of these seemingly absurd conditions, not only in terms of scenery but of actors appearing before audiences as their "real" selves. That post-mimetic condition will be a major concern of this book, but the romantics, and even the realists, still remained committed to mimesis, though their concept was moving closer to the emergence of the real in performance.

Despite the romantic interest in more accurate scenic presentations, what audiences of this period actually saw in the theatre, except for the actors, remained essentially two-dimensional pieces of scenery. Unless actually required by the action, even objects like tables and chairs still remained normally painted on the backdrop. The neoclassical theatre had a long tradition of the occasional and sometimes critical use of individual chairs and tables in comedy—one thinks of the well-known table in *Tartuffe* or the chair in which Molière was stricken by his fatal illness in *Le Malade imaginaire* (a chair that still may be seen today preserved in a glass case in the bar of the theatre), but the actors of tragedy during the great years of neoclassicism performed without even these minimal scenic elements. Talma, in early nineteenth-century France, when romanticism was already in the air, began to introduce individual chairs into tragedies, and in the 1820s shocked his audiences by actually reclining on a couch in Joy's *Scylla*, an action never before seen on the tragic stage.[12]

It was really not until the middle of the century, however, that, with the growing interest in realistic depictions of bourgeois life, audiences were able to see characters like themselves moving about in rooms with the three-dimensional elements of everyday life: chairs, tables, cupboards, stools, practical instead of painted windows, and doors with real, working doorknobs. Tom Robertson, the house dramatist for Squire and Marie Bancroft in London in the 1860s, was known as the author of "cup and saucer" dramas, this descriptive phrase pointing out the extensive use of these homely, real objects, along with newspapers, knitting, and similar materials from everyday life. Although the provenance of such small items is not recorded, one can assume that they were on the whole real objects, obtained from the same sources as their equivalents in real life, unlike traditional stage furniture, like Talma's couch, created for stage use only in a scene shop.

With the coming of the more scrupulous realism of the late nineteenth century, to which was often given the name *naturalism*, directors more and more equated mimesis in the theatre not only with acting that attempted to reproduce the behavior of everyday life, but with a total stage environment that would place that actor in surroundings that, as Hugo suggested, necessarily were associated with and reinforced the presentation of that actor. As Zola, the leading theorist of naturalism, argued: "the physiological man of our modern tragedies demands more and more imperiously to be determined by the décor, by the milieu of which he is the product."[13] Essentially mimesis came to be equated with verisimilitude, and pioneer theatre champions of naturalism were noted as much for the "real" items on their stages (most famously, André Antoine's use of real sides of beef from a local slaughter-house) as for the everyday quality of the language, situations, and characters in the naturalistic drama itself.

The theatre artist most associated with mimesis as verisimilitude, preferably with the use of material from the real world, was the American David Belasco, many of whose most popular productions were actually created to emphasize the photographic reality of their scenery. In his autobiography, *Through the Stage Door*, Belasco comments that the searches for accurate items for his stage were "really the most interesting parts of my work." He tells of attending auction sales and haunting antique shops, of rummaging "in stores in the richest as well as the poorest sections of New York," and of dispatching agents to London, Paris, even Japan, in search of suitable authentic visual elements. His description of how he found the proper scenery for *The Easiest Way*, a popular thriller of 1909 which he wrote and directed himself, is worth quoting in full:

> I planned one of its scenes to be an exact counterpart of a little hall bedroom in a cheap theatrical boarding-house in New York. We tried to build the scene in my shops, but, somehow, we could not make it look shabby enough. So I went to the meanest theatrical lodging-house I could find in the Tenderloin district and bought the entire interior of one of its most dilapidated rooms— patched furniture, thread-bare carpet, tarnished and broken gas fixtures, tumble-down cupboards, dingy doors and window-casings, and even the faded paper on the walls. The landlady regarded me with amazement when I offered to replace them with new furnishings.[14]

This almost obsessive concern with the imitation of real life reinforced whenever possible by real-life objects faded in the theatre with the rise of the cinema, which could achieve such effects with far greater ease and flexibility, taking its camera, if need be, to an actual boarding house rather than removing and transporting its elements, or going to locations and filming elements impossible to create realistically upon a stage. As the cinematic challenge mounted, productions devoted to the detailed reproduction of the real in the Belasco style gave way to more simplified and abstract representations, often still based on external reality but moving away from such heavy reliance upon real elements from it. When Belasco-style realism enjoyed a brief revival on the Broadway stage of the early 1930s, with Sidney Kingsley's *Dead End*, Elmer Rice's *Street Scene*, and Jack Kirkland's *Tobacco Road*, the detailed verisimilitude of these productions was highly praised, but they were really the last significant examples of Belasco photographic realism on the major professional stage.

Although the use of real elements in the theatre was championed by major nineteenth century theorists from Hugo to Zola and beyond, there was very little theoretical attention given to the possible tension between the theatrical illusion and a real object. On the contrary, the conflation of verisimilitude and mimesis encouraged producers in the Antoine-Belasco tradition to feel that the introduction of such material actually increased the effect of the theatrical performance. Only within acting theory can one see a certain uneasiness about the utilization of actual material from the extra-theatrical world, and this on the part of those acting theorists following in the tradition of Diderot, who were concerned that too great a reliance upon the emotions one truly felt outside the theatre risked interfering with theatrical effectiveness. The leading French actor of the late nineteenth century, Coquelin, took this position, but the strong general interest in the theatre of the period in the reproduction of reality tended to favor the theories of Stanislavsky, which, especially as promulgated in the United States, felt that real-life emotions were not in conflict with the actor's art, but powerful raw material for it.

During the 1930s and the 1940s, important critical voices appeared that felt it important to stress the double consciousness in theatre of the real and the artificial, especially in respect to the actor. One such voice was that of Bertolt Brecht, and others were in large part members of the Prague linguistic school, especially Petr Bogatyrev, writing on the folk theatre. Neither Brecht nor Bogatyrev were particularly concerned with the actor's existence outside the theatre, but both were concerned with the importance of the audience's awareness of a separation between actor and character, and the dynamic between them—Brecht emphasizing the actor's work in creating the actor—Bogatyrev, the transformation the actor experienced in moving from a life situation to a theatrical one. When semiotic analysis began to be applied again to the theatre after the Second World War, its influence among theatre scholars spread and by the 1960s it had become the dominant theoretical methodology within theatre studies. Then the question of the live body of the actor and the sign or signs it produced onstage was again taken up and much expanded.

Semiotic analysis was devoted to a study of human communication, including the communicative functions of the arts. Individual meaning-bearing elements were referred to as signs, and one of the pioneers of semiotics, Charles Saunders Pierce, established a threefold classification of signs that became one of the foundation stones of the field. He divided signs into icons, which resembled in some way what they represented; indexes, which were related in some way to what they represented; and symbols, which were connected with what they represented only by cultural convention. Almost as soon as modern semioticians began to analyze the theatre, they remarked on the centrality in the theatre of iconic signs. Keir Elam, in the first book-length study in English on theatre semiotics, noted that in the theatre iconicity regularly appears in its most extreme form, when an element in the production is not merely "like" the thing it represents, but is in fact the same thing, or at least the same *kind* of thing as appears in the real world. Thus, a chair represents a chair, a cup and saucer a cup and saucer. Such objects, often in fact appropriated for stage use from their real-life existence, Elam noted as particularly significant in the theatre, signs that were not only iconic, but possessed what he called "iconic identity."[15] This phenomenon was probably most strikingly pointed out in the mid-twentieth-century theatre in Peter Handke's widely produced experimental piece of 1966, *Offending the Audience*. The play was presented by persons who renounced normal theatrical illusion and proposed to present the normal iconic material of theatre stripped of both iconicity and signification. "We are not representatives," they announced. "We represent nothing . . . We don't step out of our roles. We have no roles. We are ourselves." This same neutrality extends to the entire visual field: "The light that illuminates us signifies nothing. Neither do the clothes we wear signify anything. They indicate nothing."[16]

Despite occasional experimental theatre works that attempted to challenge or destabilize the operations of iconic identity (Pirandello's works are one notable example), the operations of real elements in the theatre were not given a central position in theatrical theory until the 1980s when theatre phenomenologists, headed by Bert O. States, utilized this phenomenon to distinguish their theoretical focus from that of the semioticians. States begins his short but highly influential book, *Great Reckonings in Little Rooms* by noting that for semioticians, everything onstage is a sign, that is, it is not a part of the actual world of social praxis, but refers to it in some way. Although he does not use the term, this "reference" to a reality beyond the theatrical depiction once again returns us to the operations of mimesis. However, States continues, if we approach the theatre not semiotically but phenomenologically, a very different perspective upon its components opens. We become more aware of the fact that the elements of theatre, "unlike fiction, painting, sculpture, and film" consist "to an unusual degree of things that *are* what they seem to be."[17] Later on, States summarizes his observations thus: "Theater is the medium, par excellence, that consumes the real in its realest forms: man, his language, his rooms and cities, his weapons and tools, his other arts, animals fire and water—even, finally, theater itself. Its permanent spectacle is the parade of objects and process *in transit* from environment to imagery."[18] Essential to States's argument is that this is an ongoing process. "One could define the history of theater" he argues, "especially where we find it over-throwing its own traditions—as a progressing colonization of the real world." Phenomena like live animals onstage, one of his key examples of objects "in transit," he calls nearly perfect symptoms of "the cutting edge of theatre, the bite that it takes into actuality in order to sustain itself in the dynamic order of its own ever-dying signs and images."[19]

The coming of modern realism and naturalism, attempting to present what Jean Jullien, one of Antoine's naturalist playwrights, famously described as a "slice of life," it seems that the "progressive colonization of the real world" noted by States [20] had reached its natural limits, but in the course of the twentieth century, and especially in the generation that has passed since the appearance of *Great Reckonings in Little Rooms*, a significant part of the experimental theatre of Europe and the United States has developed work that seems to indicate that the appetite of theatre for reality continues to develop, that it continues, in a number of fascinating and challenging ways, to "bite into actuality." Alain Badiou argued that the history of twentieth-century art (and of twentieth-century politics) has been dominated by a search for the real, for authenticity. In order for this to be pursued, repetition, and its coproduct, simulation, as theorized for example by Baudrillard, must be somehow interrupted.[21] Within the theatre, the primary strategy for this project, in fact extending back well before the twentieth century, has been a continuing exploration and development of that traditional theatre dynamic so well described by Bert States, the dynamic of "devouring the real in its realest forms."[22]

The phenomenological approach of States may be said to remain based upon the essentially binary relationship between the mimetic and the real as it had been articulated ever since Plato, and which has been the basis of the trajectory of these concepts I have so far been tracing. By the time States's *Great Reckonings* appeared in the mid-1980s, however, the revolutionary philosophical discourse of deconstruction, launched by Jacques Derrida and others, was providing profound challenges to this and many other long-accepted assumptions of Western thought. Among the central assertions of this new philosophic methodology was that "pure presence," the basis of the traditional "real," in fact was not real, or could not be discovered, but that all experience is always from the beginning involved in copying and imitation.[23]

The operations of theatre, so closely intertwined with representation, attracted the attention of these new theorists from the very outset, most notably in Derrida's discussions of Artaud's attacks on mimesis. Derrida points out that Artaud's attacks on mimesis, like those of Plato, continue to seek a non-mimetic grounding in a fundamental "real." Theatre and performance theorists like Elinor Fuchs[24] developed Derrida's challenge to this model with a more specific attention to theatre in the later years of the century, but the book which served as the central theoretical statement of the impact of the new theories and practice of the late twentieth century was surely the widely read and quoted *Postdramatic Theatre* (2006) of Hans-Thies Lehmann. Although only a few pages of this work are devoted to mimesis, Lehmann's approach to this subject has become a standard reference point for much subsequent writing on the subject. Lehmann's utilization of the ubiquitous theoretic prefix "post" and his general rhetoric seems to place him in an intellectual world closely related to that of theorists like Derrida and Fuchs. He argues that to understand what he calls the postdramatic theatre, we must "free ourselves" from the centrality of this term to the theatre, accepted ever since the Greeks. Although "no poetics of drama has ever abandoned the concept of action as the object of mimesis," Lehmann asserts, "the reality of the new theatre begins precisely with the fading away of this trinity of drama, imitation, and action."[25] In a later section, among the eleven "traits" of the postdramatic, Lehmann lists the disappearance of traditional mimesis and the new importance of the "real."

Subsequent considerations of the real in performance practice and theory, most notably the 2013 *Acts and Apparitions* of Liz Tomlin,[26] and, to a lesser extent, the 2012 *Trauma-Tragedy* of Patrick Duggan[27] have provided important elaborations to and modifications of Lehmann's approach. Tomlin has argued that Lehmann's postdramatic still, to a significant extent, reinscribes a traditional avant-garde binary by opposing the traditional dramatic for as mimetic of an illusory external reality, subject to the manipulations of social and cultural forces to the postdramatic, which Lehmann describes as "an intentionally unmediated experience of the real."[28]

Certainly in such distinctions as in Lehmann's often quoted phrase, the "irruption of the real" into a closed fictive universe,[29] strongly suggest an almost conventional binary of the "real" of everyday life and the mimetic university of the stage.

As early as 1996 Andrew Quick warned that with the theory and practice of such emerging experimental forms as performance art and live art there was often an attempt to resist the workings of representation, "while somehow being or representing 'the real' itself." Such attempted framings of the real or of reality, Quick warned, were "extremely limited and may, indeed, be unwittingly contradictory."[30] In the two decades since that warning, his caution has become more and more generally accepted among writings about representation and the real in the theatre. Stephen Bottoms, to give only a single important example, has insisted that "placed within the frame of art, the 'real' is always already representational, and the 'self' always already a characterization."[31]

In terms of the actual operations of the theatre itself and of the experience of those operations, however, this has not removed the real from critical attention, but in fact has opened a more complex and nuanced view of the many ways that the idea of the real circulates through the field of representation. Cormac Power's 2008 study of presence in the theatre provides an excellent example of the potential of these new insights. As we move away from the rather simplistic view of theatre as an activity that is particularly concerned with presenting the real, or according to Power's formulation, the "present," the possibility is then open to us, in the words of Tomlin: "to investigate, destabilize or expose the complex levels of presence which make up the theatre event."[32] Thus Power's evocative argument concludes that "it is the very potential of theatre to put presence *into play* that enables us to consider the importance of theatre as an art form that can allow us to reflect upon and question the construction of 'reality' in the contemporary world" (emphasis in the original).[33]

In the chapters that follow we will consider the utilization of real material from a variety of historical periods, demonstrating that the utilization of such material, as Bert States noted, has been a defining characteristic of theatre from its very beginnings. We will also find in earlier periods many cases of dramatic practice that utilized strategies Lehmann would seemingly characterize as postdramatic. What distinguishes most recent experimentation is not the experimental approaches themselves, but the much more widespread and self-conscious utilization of them combined with an undermining of the traditional distinctions between the real and the representation. Audiences have often been taken out of the theatre, traditionally a space devoted to illusion, and placed in situations where they are encouraged to view objects and persons around them as the manifestations that can only be understood though the process of representation, which is at the foundation of human consciousness. Both Europe and the United States have, at the turn of the twenty-first century, witnessed productions in which audience/participants were not given access to the controlled environments of traditional theatres, but, in some cases, simply conducted to a particular location or locations and invited to view the activity there, presumably not consciously staged, as performance. It may be that they are given no information as to whether that the activities that they witness are in fact staged for their benefit, partially staged, or indeed what they appear to be—the operations of everyday reality in those places. In the final chapter we will examine a number of key examples of this process.

A calculated ambiguity between the real and the mimetic has been a major strategy of much experimental theatre of the twentieth century from Pirandello onward, but mere ambiguity is no longer, if it ever really was, at the center of current performance experiments with reality. The concern is rather to demonstrate that the real and the represented are not a set binary, but are the products of human consciousness and ways of seeing and encoding. A number of theorists, including Lehmann, have spoken of the undecidability of what may be real in modern performance, but even that expression still contains resonances of a binary that would allow a decision. A better approach is probably that of Power, with the idea of multiple *levels* of reality at play, or Duggan's lovely phrase "mimetic shimmering," suggesting not an either or of the real and the mimetic, but a constantly shifting awareness of the construction and deconstruction of the "real" world around us. This does not at all mean that the theatre has moved beyond a fascination with the tension between the real and the representative. Like all human activities, it offers in any period, and particularly in the present, a layering of strategies and assumptions from many sources and historical times. Within an important part of its contemporary activity, however, especially in that realm of the experimental theatre that has been most influenced by postmodern and poststructuralist theory, theatre has not rejected the ideas of mimesis and the real, but it has moved those terms out of the realm of verifiable objectivity and into the realm where the theatre actually takes place, within the infinitely complex and variable scene of human perception and understanding. Here the traditional contrasted binary of the two terms becomes a constantly shifting field of differing relationships.

CHAPTER I

Verbatim

The theorists who have given the most specific attention to theatre's particular utilization of material from the real world have
been the phenomenologists and, as I noted in the introduction,
Bert O. States in particular stressed the art's ongoing attraction to
"the real in its realist forms." In his listing of the materials from
the world of experience utilized by theatre, States mentions language, and includes a few provocative comments on the somatic
"field of sound" created by an actor's presentation of lines,[1] but
his work *Great Reckonings in Little Rooms*, like the work of phenomenological theorists in general, concerns itself primarily with
physical objects—the human body and the physical world that
surrounds it. States indeed begins his study with the famous definition of art by the Russian formalist Viktor Shklovsky: "Art exists that one my recover the sensation of life; it exists to make
one feel things, to make the stone *stony*."[2]

Words, however, in addition to whatever somatic impressions
given them by an actor's delivery, are even more fundamentally
material from the real world, however insubstantial, appropriated
from that world for stage use like almost everything seen and heard
on the stage. Actually, linguists have had more to say about this
appropriation than phenomenologists, and doubtless the best-
known comments on the matter come from J. L. Austin. These
comments make up a part of Austin's observations on performativity, which have been so influential in modern performance theory.
In his central text, *How to Do Things with Words*, Austin specifically excludes "utterances spoken on stage" (and in other fiction)
from his analysis since they are "parasitic" upon real-life speech

acts and "in a peculiar way hollow and void,"[3] Of course, as Sean Zwagerman points out in his study of women's humor and performativity: "We do not take the actor who says, 'Master Shallow, I owe you a thousand pound,' to have truly committed himself to a debt,"[4] but noting that this statement does not function performatively in the non-fictive world does not remove its reality as a real linguistic utterance, as Derrida pointed out. It is also worth noting, given the influence of Austin's observation, that even onstage not all performative utterances are hollow. This same play opens with the request by Rumor for the audiences to "Open your ears," a performative if there ever was one, and addresses to the audience have for centuries made similar requests.[5]

In fact, a direct performative appeal to the audience's attention at the opening of a play or for their applause at the ending are only two especially striking examples of the vast array of types of speech given directly from actor to audience, permeating the walls of the fictive world, but, most important for my concern here, necessarily utilizing real words from the real world.[6]

Traditionally, direct addresses to the audience are presumed to originate in the fictive world inhabited by the character who delivers them, but this division has often been eroded by prologues and epilogues, especially when they are delivered, as was often the case, for example in the English Restoration, by an actor or actress in costume, but no longer in character.

Although this long-standing convention of actor/audience address challenges Austin and Searle's removal of performative discourse from the theatre, stage speech in general clearly has, for much of theatre history, shared what Austin characterizes as a certain "hollowness." In this, it may be compared to the physical movements and gestures of the body. These also are "parasitic upon" social and cultural practice outside the theatre, and are meant to be interpreted in the same way. The fictive world of the theatre, despite the styles and conventions of different periods and cultures, has been generally assumed to be basically congruent with the world its audiences inhabit. Lacking the physical reality of the actor, words, though also brought in from the world outside the theatre, cannot in the normal course of things, reveal that world by some sort of disruption of the fictive world, as when an actor suffers an actual physical injury.[7]

Thus bringing human speech, with its grammar and syntax, into the theatre, while a central feature of the art, rarely, if ever, calls attention to itself as a borrowing from the "real" world. If, however, all or part of the theatrical text is recognized as coming from that world, then the situation is very different, and the steady development of this use of language in theatre has become more and more important in modern times, particularly during the past century. The long-standing convention of the "play within a play" often presented audiences with actors reading from already-prepared texts, but despite Shakespeare's famous observation that "all the world's a stage," the constant disguising and internal theatrics of his plays never seek to remind the audience that Hamlet or Rosalind are themselves actually reciting prewritten material. That further step was taken by romantic dramatists like Tieck and experimental modernists like Pirandello, whose characters could and did step back from their presumed script, comment upon it, or even outright reject it. It may be that at least some of the early audiences of these innovative dramatists accepted these metatheatrical tricks and assumed that they were seeing a breakthrough of the real onto the stage, but surely no thoughtful theatregoer was fooled for long, and today such devices have been thoroughly absorbed into the operations of the theatrical illusion.

Much more effective in modern times has been a distinctly different way of calling the audience's attention to the fact that the words being spoken onstage have, in fact, like the bodies of the actors, been brought into the theatre from the outside world and incorporated into the constructed world of the theatre. This is the central feature of what has been most commonly called the documentary theatre, although it has appeared during the past century in a variety of forms and bearing a variety of names. The first clear example of this type of drama was the 1925 *In Spite of Everything!* by Erwin Piscator, who created a new sort of theatrical experience based on contemporary news reporting and designed to reflect current social reality for its audiences. The revue format in which this material was presented was totally in harmony with current artistic expression in Russia, clearly related to Meyerhold's interest in circus and revue forms and even more closely to Eisenstein's "Montage of attractions," which appeared only two years before. Although all of these artists were devoted to work that would reflect the evolving political scene, only Piscator focused on the presentation of actual historical documents. A statement of 1928 expresses his motivation clearly: "It is not theatre we want, but reality. Reality is still the biggest theatre."[8]

This search for a more effective representation of the "real" can, of course, be traced in European theatre back through naturalism and realism, to romanticism, a century before, but the use of "real" documentary material onstage was a new focus. As Attilio Favorini observed, the earlier movements retained the age-old "emphasis on the clash of personalities" as well as the psychological concerns of realistic drama.[9] "Of what import to us are the problems of half-insane people," said Piscator, in a world where "real shocks spring from the discovery of a gold field, from petroleum production, and from the wheat trade!"[10] Looking forward rather than backward, Piscator's rejection of psychological and character concerns make his work an early example of what Hans-Thies Lehmann has called "postdramatic theatre."[11]

Although Piscator is widely considered the creator of "documentary" theatre, the presentation onstage of material from the real world, especially from newspapers, became widespread during the Russian Revolution. The Soviet living newspaper (*zhivaia gazeta*) was created by Red Army units to provide information on the current political situation to illiterate comrades. It was an eclectic mix—part broadsheet, part music hall, part political rally. Along with such entertainments as mock trials, pageants, and puppet shows, it became important tools of the new regime to present its political messages.[12]

Despite the generic title of *living newspaper*, the majority of groups associated with this term, like the Moscow Blue Blouse, did not in fact present much if any actual verbatim material onstage. Rather, they used current news stories as the basis for theatricalized commentary on them, not unlike an important part of the earlier British music hall or German cabaret traditions. A certain part of the avant-garde, however, saw the use of actual verbal texts as critical. This was a central concern of the so-called factographers (*Faktoviki*), who advocated the use of concrete details from daily life as the basis for a new and utilitarian artistic form that they called a "literature of fact." Although this group was primarily interested in literature, their journal, *New Left* (*Novyi lef*), also strongly supported the living newspapers.[13]

The American living newspaper, created as part of the 1930s Federal Theatre Project (FTP), generally based its work on news items as did the Blue Blouse, rather than present actual texts from the news, but its first creation, *Ethiopia*, prevented from ever opening by government pressure, was a notable exception. It was composed almost entirely of verbatim excerpts from speeches of world leaders on Mussolini's 1935 invasion of that country. When the Federal Theatre requested a transcript of a Roosevelt speech for the project, however, government officials, while allowing the use of the words, forbade them to be delivered by any actors representing actual political figures, a somewhat arbitrary distinction perhaps, but one that caused the FTP to withdraw the play and refrain from further experiments of this sort.

The FTP's troubles with the government were far from over, however, and after four turbulent years, its politically engaged productions proved too radical for an increasingly conservative government to support. Not until the 1960s, with a resurgence of interest in theatre dealing with current social problems, did documentary drama, and verbatim material, again make an important contribution to the American stage.

In part, this was inspired by a new interest in documentary theatre in Germany, led by Rolf Hochhuth, Heinar Kipphardt, and Peter Weiss, in works often directed, most appropriately, by Piscator, who had returned to Germany after a twenty-three-year exile in the United States. Their work was part of a general reaction in the arts in the 1960s against the conscious historical blindness of the Adenauer regime concerning recent German history. All were concerned with using the stage as a kind of tribunal, as Schiller had advised, but it was Weiss, the chief theoretician of the movement, who made the most extensive use of verbatim materials, particularly in *The Investigation* (1965), with a script taken from the Frankfurt war-crime trials, and *Vietnam Discourse* (1968), with a second act composed entirely of political speeches, in the manner of *Ethiopia*.

In his manifesto "Fourteen Propositions for a Documentary Theatre," Weiss insists that "The documentary theatre shuns all invention. It makes use of authentic documentary material which it diffuses from the stage, without altering the contents, but in structuring the form." The final phrase is a key one. In Weiss's view, documentary theatre was a clearer picture of reality than the documents it utilized, since it revealed more clearly the truth hidden within "the inchoate mass of information which constantly assails us from every side."[14] Predictably, those who disagreed with Weiss's leftist political position, claimed that this "structuring" distorted the text to favor his interpretation of reality, a charge regularly leveled at politically oriented documentary drama, which, from Piscator onward, has been almost exclusively political and almost exclusively left-leaning.

It is worth noting that one of Weiss's two major documentary dramas distinctly looks back to the past, to Piscator and *Ethiopia*, while the other looks toward the future, when the transcript of court trials would become one of the major found sources for such theatre. One might argue that the courtroom drama is one of the oldest dramatic forms, going back to the beginnings of Western drama and to the epic trial that concludes Aeschylus's *Oresteia*. The arguments and counterarguments and the built-in conflict give such material a natural dramatic form, and Shakespeare's *Merchant of Venice* is only one of the many major plays found throughout theatre history that have a court trial at their center. The form enjoyed a particular popularity during the late twentieth century, however, sometimes in works with a clear political message (*The Crucible* and *Inherit the Wind*), and other times when the interplay and tensions of the trial itself were central (*Witness for the Prosecution* and *Twelve Angry Men*). Although many of these were inspired by actual criminal cases, Piscator's was the first to take actual trial records as a dramatic text, creating a model that would be widely followed. The form was introduced to the United States in 1970 by Donald Freed's *Inquest*, which touched off a firestorm of controversy by returning, at this turbulent period, to the always controversial trial of Julius and Ethel Rosenberg.

In an essay published with the text of this play, Freed called *Inquest* a "Theatre of Fact," in that "every word is taken from primary sources. At its most lunatic there is not an invented word in the entire play."[15] Like earlier creators of documentary theatre, Freed saw the use of verbatim material as a strategy for revealing truth suppressed by the people in power, but in 1970 he saw this revelation in a different context than his predecessors. Looking back on the late 1960s and citing Artaud's *The Theatre and Its Double*, first published in English in 1958 and a key manifesto for writers in the following decade, Freed cited Artaud's Theatre of Cruelty as a necessary corollary in contemporary times to the Theatre of Fact. Having been passive to authoritarian repression in the Rosenberg era, America must now suffer a replay of that repression in such manifestations as the Trial of the Chicago Seven, opening the year before *Inquest*. For Freed, exposure of the real onstage seeks to force audiences to confront repressed truths whose repression continues to afflict them. Combining Weiss and Artaud, he proclaims that: "What you see really happened; that is fact. Now you must let it happen to you, that is existential or moral cruelty. You who were passive and did not choose when you had the chance now must undergo everything twice."[16] To break this cycle, Freed argues, the theatre must return to its traditional role of purgation, in which function the presentation of the real becomes critical.

After *Inquest*, the presentation of courtroom documents became one of the most favored forms of documentary drama, especially in the United States. *The Trial of the Catonsville Nine*, written by Father Dan Berrigan, a leader of the anti-war movement and produced in 1971, while Berrigan was still in prison, about his own court experience, is a central example of such work. I remember also in the late 1960s seeing several stagings of Brecht's testimony before the House Committee on Un-American Activities, a text widely circulated among leftist groups as an example of right-wing suppression of the arts. Although the trope of a miscarriage of justice can be found in all of these plays and that of a continuing legacy of suffering and inequality in most, such plays normally show the protagonist or protagonists as victims of an oppressive system. Dan Isaac, in a 1971 study of several recent examples of the form, concludes that "Every instance of Theatre of Fact, beginning with the Living Newspapers in the thirties, dramatizes the victimization of the individual by the State."[17] In an emotional sense, this theatre continues to the long-established Western tradition of the martyr play.

Almost invariably, despite the use of real found material in these plays, their critics accused them of distorting this material by selectivity and lack of contextualization. These misgivings were given powerful theoretical support during the 1970s and 1980s by poststructuralist theorists such as Derrida, who in dissolving the boundary between fiction and fact also seriously undermined the truth claims of found material from real life. A closely related undermining came from historian Hayden White, who argued in his 1973 *Metahistory: The Historical Imagination in Nineteenth-Century Europe* and related works that historical writing is not essentially different from literary writing in many ways, sharing the strong reliance on narrative for meaning, thus ruling out the possibility for truly objective history, and, of course, eroding the similar objective claims of theatre utilizing material from the real world.[18]

The influence of this new view of historical fact did not lessen theatre's interest in verbatim material, but opened a different perspective on it, so that instead of the presumed "objective" presentation of such material from the living newspaper through *The Trial of the Catonsville Nine*, certain performing groups shifted their attention to a study of the questions raised by White and others of how historical material was selected and interpreted.

One of the first, and most radical theatrical reflections of the challenges of poststructuralism to traditional epistemology and ontology was the American Wooster Group, which, since its emergence onto the critical scene around 1985, has been regularly characterized as the premiere, if not the only American theatre devoted to strategies derived from poststructuralism and deconstruction.[19] As David Savran pointed out in the first extended analysis of the Wooster Group in 1988,[20] all productions of the group began with a body of found "objects" of various kinds, among them being fragments of pre-existing texts of all sorts—interviews, transcripts, earlier dramatic material, and bits of pre-recorded music, film and video. Most of this type of material can be seen in the documentary theatre tradition going all the way back to the Russian Revolution, but the way such fragments are used is here completely different. Savran compares the work of Wooster Group director Elizabeth LeCompte to that of a "maker of collages." She "takes up a found object, a fragment, that comes onto the scene without fixed meaning, and places it against other fragments," creating a fluid collection of material whose parts are never "cemented" to each other, and none of which "ever becomes a fixed center." The countless "shards" of material create "a text that remains radically plural and irreducible, a text that defies a single reading."[21]

Thus in a Wooster Group production like *L.S.D.*, verbatim material is used in a manner almost totally opposed to that of the traditional documentary theatre. In the latter, the material is presented to give audiences a more truthful and accurate picture of their social and political surroundings than that provided by the media or by generally held assumptions. No such truth claims are attached to the verbatim material utilized by the Wooster Group. On the contrary, it is presented as simple raw material for the artistic collage the company is creating, no different in value from other found or created material—fictional and factual film clips, home videos, quotations of classic dramas, and crude burlesque entertainments, even from their own previous productions. The privileged position given to verbatim material in the documentary theatre is here totally absent; it is simply part of the mix used to shape the production. This is not to say that its inclusion is not important. The very fact that such "real" material is included, but *not* privileged, is directly in accord with the central poststructuralist concept that *all* reality is filtered through narrative and other structures, and that no text is in itself more transparent or reflective of true "reality" than any other. None therefore presented an orientation point for the audience, and thus the production assumed a wide variety of audience experience and interpretation, with no specific "message" being intended or desired.

Although the Wooster Group presents a particularly clear example of this dynamic, many of the documentary dramas produced toward the end of the twentieth century reflected a similar view of the constructedness and ambiguity of documentary material. Indeed, the presentation of that view often seemed more central than whatever particular political or social situation was the announced subject of the drama. A good example of this shift in the more traditional theatre is the 1992 *Unquestioned Integrity: The Hill/Thomas Hearings* by Mame Hunt. The work was largely drawn from the testimony of the confirmation hearings the previous year for Clarence Thomas to the Supreme Court, in the course of which Anita Hill created a major political uproar by accusing Thomas of sexual harassment. Such material would be ideal for a traditional documentary drama, a highly publicized trial which could be converted into a documentary martyr-play of the individual confronting an entrenched system of power. Interestingly, it would be possible to construct such a drama using verbatim materials either to present Hill or Clarence as the martyr, depending on whether the material used emphasized sexual harassment or racism.

Certainly aware of this ambiguity, but probably even more in sharing the late-twentieth-century suspicion of unmediated reality, Hunt created a drama, where, as Favorini concludes, the issue was not the determination of which side was right but rather "verification itself, the possibility of accurate recollection and reporting, and especially how credibility is fabricated in the electronic age."[22] In Hunt's own words, the dramatic core of the trial was the fact that as it progressed, "the idea that an absolute truth could ever be found, as if there is an absolute truth" clearly "fell apart," and ultimately seems to see the function of her drama as illustrating this insight.[23]

Perhaps the best-known contemporary American author of documentary drama is Moisés Kaufman, who first came to wide attention with his 1997 off-Broadway success, *Gross Indecency: The Three Trials of Oscar Wilde*. Like *Unquestioned Integrity*, this is drama based on records of hearings that involved a highly visible social concern—this time, homosexuality—a topic that since the Stonewall riots of 1969 had become a more and more open interest of the American theatre, especially with the rise of the AIDS epidemic in the 1980s. No historical figure was more widely seen as a martyr to anti-gay prejudice than Oscar Wilde, and his trial and subsequent imprisonment became emblematic of such prejudice. He seems a perfect subject for a traditional courtroom documentary presenting him as a representative martyr, like the Rosenbergs, but by the mid-1970s the erosion of trust in that style of documentary had so far eroded in the theatre that Kaufman's play much more resembles the Wooster Group *L.S.D.* than the *Trial of the Catonsville Nine*. Although the play's stage resembled a courtroom, with prosecution on one side and defense on the other, who in fact presented excerpts from the three trials, at the front of the stage was a long table with four narrators, who continuously sorted through and read from piles of books and papers in front of them, almost exactly echoing the presentation of *L.S.D.* Their material included newspaper reports, non-courtroom material from and about male prostitutes, and quotations from such figures as George Bernard Shaw and Queen Victoria and a modern (unnamed) academic pedantically discussing Wilde's sexuality in its historical context (very much like the academic explicating *Our Town* in the Wooster Group's *Routes 1 and 9*). In short, the drama is not primarily concerned with defending Wilde, but with showing how the raw materials of history, past and present, are continually interacting with each other to create both what we call the historical record and what we *think* is in the historical record—clearly a use of verbatim material much more in harmony with the historical thinking at the close of the twentieth century.

Despite the considerable attention given to the Wooster Group and to Kaufman's *Three Trials*, their reflexive approach to docudrama and emphasis upon its constructedness, despite the support of recent developments in theory, did not signal a turning way from more traditional verbatim theatre. Indeed, a new wave of such work appeared during the 1990s, especially in the United States and England. The most important precursor of this new wave was Emily Mann, whose work in the late 1970s and early 1980s clearly anticipated it and caused her to be sometimes called "the mother of documentary theatre."[24] Her playwriting debut, in 1977, was *Annulla*, the first of a particular subgenre of the documentary to which Barney Simon, director of the South African Market Theatre, gave the name "theatre of testimony."[25] Christopher Bigsby described her work as "a theatre of survivors testifying to the lives of those who did not survive and documenting the reasons why such lives were lost."[26] In such works, the verbatim words of the survivor of some devastating experience are used as the basic text. Mann was inspired by reading, during her junior year in college, transcripts from survivors of the Nazi death camps. At that point, Mann reports, she thought, "I have to talk to people. I have to get it down, to have it in their own words."[27] In the summer of 1974 she interviewed one such survivor, Annulla Allen, in London, and was so impressed by this transcript that she decided to turn it into a one-person play, which premiered at the Guthrie Theatre in Minneapolis. With Mann's work, the martyr play of the Theatre of Fact became the testimonial play, which Gary Fischer Dawson, historian of docudrama calls a "new form" of that genre, in which the source material is "private oral histories and testimonies" that "give platform to larger societal concerns in the public area."[28]

Mann's next play, *Still Life*, was based again on interviews, here with three people in Minnesota—a deeply disturbed Vietnam veteran, and his abused wife and mistress. In this study of violence in America, Mann moved even closer to presenting "real" speech: "I wanted to retain the actual rhythms of the way each person spoke, in real language, during the interviews."[29] Her third play, *Execution of Justice*, premiered in Louisville in 1984 and presented on Broadway in 1986, relied again on interviews, this time taken from a whole community, in reaction to the murder of Mayor Harvey Milk of San Francisco in 1978, as well as on transcripts from the subsequent highly controversial trial, resulting in extensive riots.

A prominent contributor to contemporary documentary drama in general and interview-based drama in particular is Anna Deavere Smith. As early as 1978, when she was a teacher at Carnegie Mellon University, Smith hit upon the idea of expanding the work in her acting classes by asking her students to interview people in the street and then reenact the resulting testimonials. Although so far as I know Smith has not suggested any particular inspiration for this idea, it may well have come from the rapidly growing interest in oral history during that decade, and perhaps even specifically from a 1978 musical based on one of the classics of that movement, *Working*, by Studs Terkel, a bestselling book published in 1974 and composed entirely of Terkel's interviews with working people. Its aptly descriptive subtitle was "People Talk About What They Do All Day and How They Feel About What They Do."[30] Whatever her inspiration, Smith decided in the early 1980s to create a cycle of "real life" performance pieces, based on such material, which began with *On the Road: A Search for American Character* (1983) and *Aye, Aye, I'm Integrated* (1984).

The piece that brought Smith national and international attention was the next in this series, *Fires in the Mirror*, in 1992. Although it built upon Smith's earlier work, it difficult not to imagine that further inspiration came for the testimonial dramas of Emily Mann, and especially from *The Execution of Justice*, which was presented on Broadway in 1986. Smith's work dealt with a series of bloody riots in Brooklyn in the summer of 1991, touched off when a car driven by a Hasidic Jewish man struck and killed a young Caribbean-American boy, sparking protests in which a black gang killed, in retaliation, a visiting Jewish student from Australia. Like the Tectonic Theatre Project, Smith went into the deeply troubled community and interviewed a wide variety of citizens of that community as well as civic and religious leaders, but this was a solo project. Smith collected the interviews herself, worked them into twenty-nine monologues from twenty-six different people, and then performed them herself. As Mann had suggested in *Still Life*, Smith tried to reproduce the voice, gestures, and exact verbal quality of each speaker, and thanks to her extensive notes and powers of mimicry, she dazzled audiences with her transformation into a wide range of individuals, some prominent figures already familiar to those audiences. She continued this approach with equal success in *Twilight: Los Angeles, 1992*, and continues to present one-woman shows based on interview material, though connected through more general themes, such as attitudes toward death and dying (*Let Me Down Easy*, 2008) and women and the legal system (*The Arizona Project*, 2009).

In their second and most famous docudrama, *The Laramie Project* (2000), Moisés Kaufman and the Tectonic Theatre joined in this new focus on interviews as dramatic text. A notorious real-life crime was at the heart of this work—the homophobic murder of University of Wyoming student Matthew Shepard in Laramie, Wyoming, in 1998. Instead of assembling material from local records and police reports in the manner of most documentary of the previous century, the Tectonic Theatre created their own originary text. Five weeks after Shepard's death, they went to Laramie and over the next year conducted over 200 interviews with townspeople. Out of this material they created their 2000 play, one of the most widely performed plays in America over the next decade, and also produced in other theatres around the world.

In 2008, Kaufman and others returned to Laramie to survey if and how reactions had changed over the decade, re-interviewing persons from the first visit, as well as one of Shepard's killers, now in prison. By this time, Kaufman and the project had gained such visibility that the new work was given its New York premiere not off-off-Broadway, like the original play, but in one of the city's most prestigious venues, the Brooklyn Academic of Music, which ran the two plays in repertory in February 2013.

Elin Brockman, writing on "Ideas and Trends" for the *New York Times* in May 1999, presented a theory for the new popularity of reality-based theatre. She saw the success of the interview dramas of Anna Deavere Smith as part of a "headlong rush toward reality" in the arts in general. The arts "are no longer imitating life," she argued, but "are appropriating it." The "obvious reason" she suggested, with the "sheer scale of current events, amplified by the 24-hour magnifying mirror of television," making "even the worst catastrophe feel unreal." Thus, "in order to react, jaded audiences need reality in larger, stronger concentrations."[31] The "headlong rush" toward verbatim material even touched that most unlikely of American theatre forms—the Broadway musical. This same spring saw the opening at the St. James of *The Civil War*, a musical extravaganza with a libretto drawn from letters, diaries, and historical documents.

The next project of the Tectonic Theatre after *The Laramie Project* moved in a different direction, but one that had also been anticipated by Emily Mann in her first work, *Annulla. I Am My Own Wife*, premiered in 2003, was a one-man play by Doug Wright also drawn from interviews, but this time from interviews with a single person, the German transvestite Charlotte von Mahlsdorf, who survived the Nazi and Communist regimes. Closely related to this kind of interview play was the staging of material of an individual's diary, the classic example being the 1955 dramatization of the diary of Holocaust victim Anne Frank by Frances Goodrich and Albert Hackett. The author and the subject matter of this play became so much a part of twentieth-century consciousness that its contribution to the docudrama tradition has not been much remarked, but it did open another source of found material to the theatre. Doubtless the best-known example is Alan Rickman's *My Name is Rachel Corrie*, presented at London's Royal Court Theatre in 2005. The play told the story of the young American student killed by an Israeli tank in Palestine in 2003, and was drawn from her diaries and e-mails. Although a considerable success in London, its planned transfer to the New York Theatre Workshop had to be cancelled due to protests from Jewish groups.[32]

My Name is Rachel Corrie appeared as part of a new wave of verbatim theatre internationally. In 2002, Teatr.doc introduced modern documentary theatre to Moscow, and one of its founders, Hamburg-born Georg Genoux, took the new form a decade later to Sofia, Bulgaria, where his Red House Center, specializing in this sort of work, has become the leading experimental theatre in the country. England and the United States, however, remained the major centers for such work in the early twenty-first century. Central to this development in England was the series of "tribu-nal plays," presented by Nicolas Kent at London's Tricycle The-atre. This highly influential and honored series began in 1993 with Richard Norton-Taylor and John McGrath's *Half the Pic-ture*, whose text was largely drawn from records of a governmen-tal inquiry the previous year into clandestine British arms ship-ments to Iraq. In an intriguing cycle of real to theatrical to real, this play was the first ever to be presented in the Houses of Parlia-ment, where some attendees could hear their own words reflected back to them.

The tribunal plays were central to the Tricycle repertoire and a significant part of the London theatre scene through the rest of Kent's term as artistic director, which ended in 2012. They repre-sented in important ways a revival of the strategies and even the leftist political orientation of the docudramas of the 1960s, per-haps nowhere more clearly than in the 1996 *Nuremberg*, created for the fiftieth anniversary of those trials. Norton-Taylor was listed not as author but as editor (a practice often followed in tri-bunal works) and, just as Peter Weiss had done for *The Investiga-tion* thirty years before, Norton-Taylor assembled his text from the court transcripts, which ran to twenty-three volumes.[33] The following year Kent himself worked testimony from The Hague trial of war crimes from the former Yugoslavia, presented as *Sre-brenica*. In 1999 came Norton-Taylor's *The Colour of Justice*, drawn from the transcripts of a public hearing concerning a racist murder in southeast London.

A major shift in the textual material of the tribunal plays occurred in the new century with the 2004 docudrama, *Guantanamo*, created, significantly, neither by Kent nor Norton-Taylor but by a journalist and novelist (Victoria Brittain and Gillian Slovo) commissioned by Kent "to create a verbatim play based on interviews" of the prisoners (five of them British) and others involved with the U.S. prison at Guantanamo.[34] The Tricycle's own publicity noted the change this represented: "Instead of seating [*sic*] in a courtroom, listening to evidence and editing the transcripts, the show's authors . . . have had to seek out their own witnesses."[35] Unlike Smith, but rather more in the fashion of the Tectonic theatre, this production used different actors for the different interviewees, who presented the words of these interviewees, but did not "theatricalize" them, as Smith did. As the *Economist* review noted: "The performers . . . don't 'act' the roles with the sort of embellishments common to stage performance; instead, they function as conduits of a very specific sort, giving voice to a series of Kafkaesque tales that prove doubly unsettling by being true."[36]

Following this, both approaches to found texts were utilized. In 2005, Norton-Taylor "edited" *Bloody Sunday* with archival material from a 1998 official inquiry into an army attack on civil rights demonstrators, and in 2011 Gillian Slovo's *The Riots* dealt with civil disturbances in the United Kingdom that August, creating a text from interviews with politicians, police, community leaders, and citizens and presenting their testimony in a manner strongly reminiscent of Anna Deavere Smith and even more of the Tectonic's *Laramie Project* a decade before.

Probably the dramatist best known for contributions to this new wave of docudrama in Britain is not any of the tribunal dramatists, however, but David Hare. Hare was already a well-established politically engaged dramatist when, in 1998, he departed from his previous, essentially traditional style to present as his solo acting debut, a monologue, *Via Dolorosa*, recounting his journey the previous year through Israel and Palestine and including quotations from people he met in both places. In doing so, he was building upon a subgenre of documentary theatre that had developed particularly in the United States during the 1970s and 1980s, and which was there intimately tied to feminism and subsequent movements interested in using the theatre to explore questions of identity and identity formation. Many of the leaders in the performance art of that period (such as Annie Sprinkle, Rachel Rosenthal, Ron Athey, Spalding Gray, and Tim Miller) specialized in monologues that were or claimed to be authentic transcripts of their personal life experiences.[37]

Via Dolorosa proved to be Hare's only work of that type, although it began his interest in the utilization of verbatim material onstage. In a 2002 *Guardian* interview, Hare argued that a major shift was taking place in public taste, away from fiction and its contrivances toward biography and real events. Theatre, he asserted, needed to adapt to this shift, citing as an example the most "impressive" play recently produced in London, the Tricycle *Colour of Justice*.[38] Indeed, Hare's next work suggested the tribunal plays, but with a subject and presentational style closer to that of the living newspapers. For *The Permanent Way* (2003), Hare and his actors, in the manner of the Tectonic Theatre Project, interviewed people involved with the privatization of the British railways in the 1990s. Hare collated and edited the interviews, but relied upon them to make their own statement. In the words of one of his actors: "He puts in very, very little bridging material. The play is really one statement after another. He hasn't exactly written it, he collated it."[39] The interpretation of the material suggested the theatricalized reality of Anna Deavere Smith. As director Max Stafford-Clarke reported: "The actors had to become the character they had interviewed. They had to enact, perform before the others, what and whom they had found. They weren't allowed just to report."[40]

Hare's subsequent dramas remained strongly political, and often contained material from spoken or published sources. They have often be called docudramas, but they are much more fictionalized than most such works, not infrequently having a truth-seeking protagonist who collects material on some matter of social concern. In a 2006 critique of recent British documentary theatre in general, and Hare in particular, Stephen Bottoms condemned their move back toward an unquestioned acceptance of an extra-theatrical reality, and called for a return to the more self-conscious, reflexive use of such material in works like *L.S.D.* and *Gross Indecency.*

He speculated that the current popularity of documentary drama in England might be because "most Britons still believe (somewhat gullibly?) in the underlying truth/reality of the news." By contrast this genre has not flourished in the United States, where can be found "a profound distrust of the news media in general."[41] Somewhat surprisingly, Hare's 2004 *Stuff Happens*, a central example of Bottoms's attack, was basically a discussion of how the media was manipulated by those in power. A simpler explanation of the greater popularity of such work in England, I propose, is that the serious British theatre has been vastly more concerned with sociopolitical matters than that of the United States ever since 1956, and the contemporary interest in documentary drama is a part of that interest.

The witness or testimonial drama, based not upon written records but on interviews, so prevalent after 2000, was anticipated, as were many elements in contemporary "found" theatre experiments, by the early experiments of the Wooster Group, particularly *Rumstick Road* (1977).

The first works presented by the Wooster Group drew important inspiration from autobiographical material provided by Spalding Gray, but such material, like other physical and textual material used by the group, was rarely used directly, but as a source for improvisational inspiration. That was the first use of the taped interviews with three family members that Gray brought to the group in 1976. In the finished performance, however, parts of these tapes were actually played, along with recording of a telephone conversation Gray had with his mother's psychiatrist, who was not warned that he was being recorded. The use of such private material, without the knowledge or permission of those being recorded led to the first, but by no means the last, public controversy over the group's work. The play was withdrawn from Obie nominations and Michael Feingold wrote in the *Village Voice:* "I'd like to register a vehement protest against using private documents and tapes in this kind of public performance."[42]

In the 1980s Gray turned his focus toward another blending of theatre and reality by developing the series of autobiographical monologues that he continued until his death in 2004. He also however continued to explore the possibilities of the interview in his own unique way. As early as 1981 he tried out an ad-lib piece called *Interviewing the Audience* while on tour in Amsterdam. He would call audience members onto the stage and ask them about their experience on the way to the theatre. He continued to refine and perform this experiment throughout the rest of his career. Writer Francine Prose called it one of her favorite pieces and reported that in it Gray was able to "discover the zeitgeist of an entire city or region of the country from the kinds of stories its citizens told, and their willingness to tell them."[43]

It was thus Gray who removed interview material from its long-standing association with witnesses to significant public events, and presented it simply as a fragment of everyday life. Anna Deavere Smith, it should be remembered, asked her students as an exercise to go out into the community, record everyday conversations, and then re-create them in the classroom as an exercise in recall and impersonation, but she did not develop, as Gray did, theatrical pieces from this kind of material.

In its continuing colonization of reality, however, the theatre has in more recent years begun to base performances on more everyday texts—interviews, conversations, and e-mails from persons not involved with major public events, crimes, or social movements. Probably the best known example of such work is that of the Nature Theater of Oklahoma, which in the first decade of the new century challenged the position of the Wooster Group as the best-known American experimental theatre company on the international scene.

The Nature Theater was founded in 1905 by Pavol Liska and Kelly Copper. Their mission statement places them at the heart of modern interest in theatrical utilization of elements of the "real" world: "we use the readymade material around us, found space, overheard speech and observed gesture."[44] Their dance/theatre piece *No Dice* (2008), strongly influenced by the chance aesthetics of John Cage, has a text culled from more than 100 hours of telephone conversations that Liska recorded over the course of several months. The company first gained major public attention with its 2010 *Romeo and Juliet*, for which Liska and

Copper called thirty friends and asked them to recount what they could remember of Shakespeare's play. The comically garbled responses were then performed as a series of monologues by a male and female actor. The culmination of the Nature Theater's work (as of 2014, when this is written) is the four part *Life and Times*, presented at New York's Public Theatre. It was hailed in the *New Yorker* as "a masterpiece" by Hilton Als, who compared its utilization of the English language to the experiments of Faulkner and Gertrude Stein.[45] These first four episodes lasted eleven hours, and another fourteen episodes were promised for the future. The text is a transcript of a series of telephone conversations with a company member, Kristin Worrall, detailing her memories of growing up on the Eastern Seaboard. One may be reminded of the Wooster Group's utilization of the Eastern Seaboard recollections of Spalding Gray, but the contrast is striking. In the early Wooster Group productions these recollections were only starting points for improvisations, and later, when Gray began performing his autobiographical monologues, these were cast in the polished and literate phrases of a natural storyteller. Worrall's words , however, are an exactly reproduced slice of current American speech, filled with pauses, fillers, ahems, ahas, and what-was-I-talking about digressions. The closest previous approach to this kind of speech was the monologues of Anna Deavere Smith, but even they were far more edited, and, moreover, devoted to material of public interest. *Life and Times* for the first time brings onstage verbatim material from everyday life in all of its complexity and banality. It is difficult to imagine that verbatim theatre could come closer to the speech of real life than this.

CHAPTER 2

Who's There?

Although any physical object in the theatre can be "borrowed" from the "real" world outside the theatre, clearly among these objects the actor traditionally holds not only the most prominent place but also the one in which the negotiation between the real external world and the theatre's fictive world is the most clear. This is because of the audience's awareness, even when repressed, that alone among these objects the actor has a consciousness, a knowledge that he or she simultaneously exists in both of these worlds. This is why animals onstage provide such a source of tension, sometimes pleasant, sometimes not, since they bring to the stage an uncompromised reality that can never been completely under the control (as can a real chair) of either the actors' or the audience's imaginary world.

Much recent work in the field of developmental psychology has been devoted to the importance of imitation to the learning and transmission of human culture.[1] An important part of cognitive development for all children is play, and an important part of play is the conscious creation of fictive worlds for exploring new possibilities. In play, a banana becomes a telephone, and a child can become a cowboy or an astronaut. Such role-playing is often performed in a group, which readily accepts the "rules" of belief and disbelief. "Let's pretend that we are robbers and you are the police." That same sort of game, familiar to almost all children from early childhood, is carried on into theatre, where the game of "let's pretend" is a long-familiar one.

Even so, it is striking in how much of the world's theatre, a great deal of effort has been undertaken seemingly to guard against the threat of the breakthrough of the underlying real. "It is not for nothing," Richard Southern observed, "that the one symbol of theatre which above all others has come to be accepted through the work is a mask. What does a mask do to the man? . . . it takes away the person we know," allowing "the assumption of the personality" of someone we do not.[2] Although a growing interest in closer imitation of everyday life has enormously diminished this characteristic of the theatre for most of the history of the genre and in most parts of the world, the actor's body has been presented in such a way as present him as the inhabitant of a world distinctly different from our own. The real bodies of the actors in the Greek theatre, the foundation of this art in the West, were completely concealed by masks, wigs, long robes, padded bodies, and elevated shoes, so that they appeared as larger-than-life iconic figures. The Japanese Noh, occupying a similar centrality among Asian forms, also traditionally employs masks, wigs, and elaborate, highly stylized costumes. Other major Asian forms, such as the Chinese Opera or the Kathakali of India, do not use masks, but traditionally employ elaborate facial makeup that removes their performers as far from the appearance of reality as the most elaborate mask could do. Here, too, the appearance of the face is supplemented by elaborate and ornate costume and headdress.

Despite the popularity of the masked commedia dell'arte in the West, the covering of the actor's face by a mask as in the Noh or by colorful abstract design as in the Chinese Opera or the Kathakali, did not generally characterize the Western theatre after the classic period. From the Renaissance through the eighteenth century, however, the body of the actor was often presented, especially in the more highly regarded genres of tragedy and opera, in costumes almost as stylized and as far from the dress outside the theatre as the ornate robes of the classic Asian stages. Male protagonists invariably wore ornate plumed helmets, a practice that began in the early seventeenth century, Roman tunics (whatever the historic period), and a spreading ballet skirt. This strange costume was worn, reports historian James Laver "in all the countries of Europe, and even in serious plays where the element of fantasy might have been supposed to be reduced to a minimum . . . the English actor Quin wore it, and he was no ballet dancer, but the most serious of tragic actors."[3] The women were equally stylized: heavily powdered faces surmounted with wigs and flowers, a deep square décolletage, a tiny waist, and a huge, elaborated decorated billowing skirt. Doubtless an important part of the motivation for such display, in both the East and the West, has been simply the pleasure of providing visual spectacle, but the widespread utilization of the practice strongly suggests an ongoing desire in most theatrical cultures to clearly separate the fictive world from the real one, and to clearly mark the inhabitants of that world as belonging entirely to it.

The end product of such an process would seem to be the creation of a world of illusion so clearly distinct from the real world of the audience's experience that an actor in a play should be accepted as existing only in that persona and in that play, but that has almost never in fact been the case. The normal state of theatre around the world is that of an established cultural institution, created by a fairly stable organization. Audiences who attend the theatre on multiple occasions, which is the normal theatre-going practice, thus will almost certainly see the same actors on repeated occasions, perhaps dozens or even hundreds of times, and so build up an idea of the actor *as actor*, inhabiting their own world instead of that of the fictive characters performed. Although the fifth-century Greek theatre was essentially an amateur one, by the Hellenistic period, acting had emerged as an established profession and along with it star performers, whose creation of each new role was haunted by the audience's previous knowledge of them as performers.[4] By the Roman era, this phenomenon had become so central to the theatre experience that ever since, Western actors have been praised by likening them to the great Roman actor, Roscius, whose fame far surpassed that of any of the fictional characters he performed. Although this phenomenon has been a central part of the theatre experience since classical times, it did not attract specific theoretical attention until the end of the twentieth century, in a pioneering study, "Celebrity and the Semiotics of Acting," by Michael C. Quinn.[5]

Quinn's discussion is grounded in the Prague semiotic school, concerned with the operation of signs and signification in human culture. Prague theorists like Otakar Zich and Jiří Veltruský, in the 1930s and 1940s, challenged the tradition binary of actor and character by introducing a third intermediate term, the stage figure, an image of the character that is created by the actor and technical means as a physical, signifying object.[6] Quinn in turn challenges this system by calling attention to how it can be disrupted by the dynamics of celebrity. "The personal, individual qualities of the performer always resist, to some degree, the transformation of the actor into the stage figure required for the communication of a particular fiction," Quinn notes, and celebrity performance "represents one case in which the personal, expressive function of acting comes into the foreground of perception."[7]

Every age in Western theatre from the Renaissance onward has produced such celebrity actors, from Burbage and Betterton through Garrick and Lekain, Bernhardt and Duse, to Olivier and Gielgud. However brilliant any of these may have been in the creation of particular roles, once their celebrity had been established, audiences were, in large part, attracted to their performances to see the actor, not the dramatic fable. It is highly important to note, however, that this attraction is not based necessarily or even primarily upon a desire to see a superior display of acting skill, but upon a desire to see a particular person. As Quinn observes, celebrity is normally "not composed of acting technique but of personal information. The first requisite for celebrity is public notoriety, which is only sometimes achieved through acting."[8] Quinn thus expands the traditional Prague triad of actor to stage figure to character by adding another "mediating element, the celebrity figure," between the actor and the stage figure.[9]

Quinn's analysis points out a major feature of the "celebrity figure," which is that it is more or less a conscious construct, partly by the audience, partly by the actor, partly by the producing organization, and in more modern times, in significant measure by the media. As soon as actors become subjects of public attention, the operations of celebrity begin to work. Stories—some real, some quite fictional—grow up about their private lives, biographies and autobiographies appear, the majority of them created less for preserving an accurate record than for adding to the image of the celebrity, and the media cater to public interest in celebrity figures by offering revelations about their private lives, resulting in the twentieth century in a vast array of magazines devoted entirely to the construction and maintenance of celebrity. Quinn argues that the celebrity figure adds another level of mediation between the real world and the stage world. It provides "an alternative reference, competing with and structuring the role of the stage figures as it promotes its own illusion." As a result, "genuine expression, like authentic selfhood, is banished to a more remote position in a more elusive reality."[10]

Unquestionably, this can be one result of celebrity performance. The casting of Madonna in the sole female role of David Mamet's *Speed-the-Plow* on Broadway in 1988 unquestionably increased box-office sales, but *Los Angeles Times* critic Dan Sullivan summed up the critical reaction to the production succinctly as "Mamet—yes. Madonna—no."[11] Still, the relationship between celebrity, theatrical illusion, and the real is extremely complex, and the negative impact Quinn rightly notes is not always in evidence. One must also acknowledge the paradox that even though celebrity seems to operate in distinct opposition to theatrical illusion, reminding the audience that the figure they are witnessing is not at all Hamlet but Laurence Olivier, not at all Camille but Sarah Bernhardt, this does not seem to interfere with audience enjoyment—indeed, celebrity actors have normally been particularly favored, praised, and enjoyed. It still strikes me as distinctly odd that even in a quite realistic play on Broadway a star actor will be applauded on entrance, even if he or she has done nothing to merit such attention except display himself/herself to the admiring public. Yet that practice does not seem to cause any serious harm to the fictional world of the stage. The best explanation of this seeming contradiction, I think, was provided by Jean Alter in his 1990 *Sociosemiotics of Theatre*. Alter suggested that the pleasure of theatre resulted from a continually operating double consciousness, processing both the referential function (the fictive world of the stage) and the performant one (the technical achievement of the actor).[12]

In any case, celebrity, despite its continual truth claims, clearly is not primarily created to bring the "real life" of the actor into the theatre—it exists for its own sake, or for the sake of influencing how the audience values the theatre experience. This is equally true whether the operations of celebrity emphasize the exceptional nature of the artist or his normality. An 1867 essay that appeared on the front page of the *New Orleans Times-Picayune* when the Italian star Adelaide Ristori was visiting that city, seems to present an intimate picture of her "real" life, but its clear purpose is less to offer truthful details than to depict her as a domestic model woman, unspoiled by her artistic triumphs:

> She arranges the economy of her own household, like any other good house wife. She watches, as a mother, over her son and daughter, and like a good wife, loves her husband.
> She personally attends to the wants of her servants, and sees they are well fed and house.
> When she travels abroad, she packs her own trunks.[13]

It is difficult to imagine that this image of the "real" Ristori as nurturing wife and mother would have done much to prepare New Orleans audiences for *Medea*, the work she presented there, yet it was received as "the most perfect production on the subject that has even been brought upon the stage" by the *Times-Picayune* on February 18, 1867. One must assume that if such advance publicity contributed at all to Ristori's reception, it was by emphasizing the artistic skill of a "really" gentle and caring woman in so convincingly portraying the savage Medea. Far from being brought into the theatre, the "real," if involved at all, served as a location of contrast.

The late nineteenth century, which began with the triumphs of Ristori and Rachel and ended with those of Bernhardt and Duse, was clearly one of the high points of celebrity acting, where Quinn's celebrity figure often, for better or worse, clearly overshadowed the stage figure. Although Quinn sees these figures as essentially in opposition, this same period also saw some remarkably successful blending of them—a further complication the use of the "real" onstage. By far the best known example of this was the international success of William F. Cody, "Buffalo Bill."

The Buffalo Bill phenomenon is an excellent example of a theatrical phenomenon growing out of the confluence of a number of powerful social forces. In the late 1860s, recovering from the devastating Civil War, the American public became fascinated with reports from the expanding frontier. At the same time, in literature and the theatre, the rising tide of realism called for stories that were, or claimed to be, true reports from that new area of interest. These interests converged on two figures that would be central in shaping the public view of the American West, Buffalo Bill Cody and Ned Buntline. Both already had an established reputation—one as a frontier warrior, the other as a writer of the enormously popular new genre of dime novels. The two careers converged in 1869 with the publication of the first installment of Ned Buntline's serial novel *Buffalo Bill, the King of the Border Men*, which was advertised, significantly, as "wildest and truest story he ever wrote."[14] Although the novel, despite this claim, was almost entirely fictional, it set the pattern for further relations between these two men, one performing real-life deeds that the other would create into modern mythology and sell to the public as reality.

The theatrical potential of Buntline's frontiersman was soon seen, and a dramatization of his novel, coauthored by Buntline, appeared in 1872. Cody, visiting New York, was provided with a private box on opening night by Buntline. When the manager of the theatre announced that the actual Buffalo Bill was in the audience, cheers went up and Cody was invited to say a few words onstage. Finding himself "standing behind the footlights and in front of an audience for the first time in my life," Cody was paralyzed with embarrassment, and totally unable to speak. Surprisingly, the manager still saw the economic potential in the situation, and that same evening offered Cody five hundred dollars a week to perform himself in the role.[15] Cody insisted he would be incapable, refused, and was soon after on his way back to Nebraska and the Indian Wars.

The seed had been sown, however, and eventually, attracted by the promised income and urged by his fellow scout Texas Jack Omohundro, who wanted to become an actor, Cody agreed to appear as the star of a new Buntline play in Chicago in December 1872. One might suppose that in the presentation of an actual play with a script and lines, Buffalo Bill would be changed from the embarrassed real human being who appeared tongue-tied before the New York audience earlier that year to some combination of Quinn's celebrity figure and stage figure, but that did not occur. Onstage, Cody reports that he could remember nothing of Buntline's text or plot. Happily, Buntline himself was also appearing onstage as himself (as was Texas Jack), and he began encouraging Cody to tell stories about his experiences, almost like an onstage interview. The work toured in this strange form, with enough success that during the rest of the 1870s Cody and Texas Jack toured regularly. In 1873 they formed the Buffalo Bill Combination, which presented works for the next decade starring themselves and other well-known frontiersmen such as Wild Bill Hickok. Never has theatre and real life been so closely intertwined. During the summer months Cody would return to the West to pursue his scouting and to fight the Indians, especially the Sioux, and during the winter he would tour with plays starring himself and presumably documenting his summer adventures. Thus, in the winter of 1876, Cody presented J. V. Arlington's *The Red Right Hand*, depicting Cody's killing of the Indian leader Yellow Hand the previous summer, offering the public what was widely accepted as a kind of documentary drama. Indeed, this achievement of Cody was so popular that Cody regularly enacted the "duel with Yellow Hand" as one of the acts in his Wild West Show. In preparation for another historical recreation, *My Cody*, the following season, Cody visited the Red Cloud Agency in South Dakota, where Indians from the Sioux Wars were being gathered into reservations, and engaged from the reservation there six Sioux Indians for his next show. From this time onward, with the blessing of the Bureau of Indian Affairs, Cody regularly recruited Indians from the reservations to give his shows another claim to reality. When he took his show to England for the Queen's Golden Jubilee in 1887, almost half of the 218 company members were Indians (a large menagerie added further realism, including 180 horses, 8 buffalo, and 10 elk).[16] Unlike the many Western white celebrities that appeared with Cody, however, Indians always appeared in generic roles, in domestic, or, more likely, aggressive situations. The best-known Indian to appear with Cody was Sitting Bull, the victor over General Custer in the most famous battle of the Sioux Wars. Sitting Bull never played himself in a conventional drama, however. In 1884 he was hired to appear in a show in New York that was essentially composed of lectures on Indian life for which Sitting Bull and his family provided a kind of authentication by sitting upstage around a teepee during the performance. The following year he was hired by Cody and they became warm friends. Cody gave Sitting Bull a privileged position among his display riders, but did not use him in any theatrical context during the warrior's single season with the company.[17]

In 1883 Cody moved away from conventional theatre, for which he never had much gift, to create a new genre, which would make him world famous—the Wild West show—combining elements of spectacle melodrama, the circus, and exhibitions of such frontier skills as horseback riding, shooting, and rope handling. Full-length plays were not a part of the new genre, but dramatic scenes offering visual spectacle were, and these included both general scenes, like the "attack on the Deadwood stage," perhaps the most famous element in the show, and restagings of actual events, like Custer's Last Stand, which remained in the show for more than a decade until it was replaced in 1899 by a re-creation of the decisive event of the Spanish-American War, the Battle of San Juan Hill, which had taken place the previous summer. Ever seeking to give authenticity to his work, Cody included sixteen veterans of the battle among his cast.[18]

At the turn of the century, the Buffalo Bill Wild West Show still dominated the field of popular entertainment, although it was being challenged by the rise of the circus. Naturally Cody's show inspired countless imitators, many of whom tried, as far as their resources would allow, to follow Cody's interest in infusing his shows with real elements—from stagecoaches to elk. The Chicago World's Fair of 1893 featured on its Midway a show called *Sitting Bull's Log Cabin*, which indeed utilized the actual cabin in which Sitting Bull was killed, and featured nine Indians, among them Sitting Bull's second in command, the almost equally renowned Rain-in-the-Face. Daniel Dorchester, an inspector with the Bureau of Indian Affairs, reported that the cast were indeed "all genuine Sioux" and included "Rain-in-the-Face, celebrated by Longfellow and reputed by some to have killed Custer."[19]

Cody was by no means an innovator in the restaging of historical events, nor with utilizing real participants of the original events in these restagings. Battle reenactments go back to ancient Rome, and the use of actual survivors in reenactments at least to the mid-seventeenth century.[20] The rise of interest both in history and in realism in the late nineteenth century inspired countless such performances, both within theatres and out of doors. Custer's Last Stand was a particular favorite, and was presented both in theatres and in outdoor celebrations, a number of which featured participants on both sides of the original battle, Sioux warriors and survivors of the U.S. 7th Cavalry Regiment.[21] By the time of the First World War the great years of the Wild West Shows were over, though their stories and images lived on in the developing film industry and their acts of physical display in the rodeo. The interest in historical accuracy carried on into the film, but was more directed toward physical location and costume than in human witnesses, who in any case were, in this media, denied physical presence.

The last great flowering of the Wild West show coincided with the first major modern vogue of historical reenactments, which became a highly popular instrument of propaganda in Revolutionary Russia. The most famous of these events, *The Storming of the Winter Palace,* was directed by one of the leading theatre directors and theorists of the Soviet era, Nicolai Evreinoff. Like the restaging in England of the Battle of Blackheath and in Belgium of the Battle Jemmapes (see note 20), this re-creation, which took place only a month after the original event and on the same site, involved both personnel and equipment that took part in that event, and which, like Cody, would return to the ongoing conflict when the reenactment was finished. In his evocation of this event, Slavoj Žižek comments: "Although this was acting and not reality, the soldiers and sailors were playing themselves. Many of them not only actually participated in the event of 1917 but were also simultaneously involved in the real battles of the civil war that were raging in the near vicinity of Petrograd, a city under siege and suffering from severe shortages of food." A contemporary commented on the performance: "The future historian will record how, throughout one of the bloodiest and most brutal revolutions, all of Russia was acting."[22] During the following century, reenactments of battles and other historical events would become a major international phenomenon and encourage further negotiations between reality and fiction. Since this phenomenon moves outside the world of traditional theatre, however, I will not pursue it further here, but return to it later in the context of audience involvement.

The rise of the film, with its far greater visual resources, was surely instrumental in the fading away of the sort of realistic historical spectacles that were so important to nineteenth-century theatre. In the new century, realism's challenge to mimesis took new forms. In the early part of the century one of the most important arose within the theatre itself, and the various challenges new experimental drama made to conventional drama, with its closed world of realistic illusion. From futurism onward, each new movement, in one way or another, sought to bring a new "reality" to the stage.[23] The best known and most influential of the many experimental artists concerned with reality's relationship to theatre was unquestionably Luigi Pirandello, to the extent that to call a work "Pirandellian" immediately suggests his particular metatheatrical experiments. Now, almost a century later, such Pirandellian devices as placing unacknowledged actors among the audiences, even at intermissions, having presumed directors or stage managers directly address the audience, actors breaking out of character, or even (apparently) really dying onstage, have become so familiar that they have in turn become immediately recognized as theatrical conventions, an excellent example of what Bert States calls the theatre "consuming" the real. Nevertheless, Pirandello's explorations into destabilizing the rigidity and fixity of art, to make it more in harmony with the fluidity and variability of life[24] can clearly be seen in such modern experimentation as the immersive theatre, to which I will return in the final chapter.

A direct descendent of such experimental movements as futurism and Dadaism were the happenings of the 1960s, where presentation of the real moved into a central position. The term *happening* was coined by Allen Kaprow in 1959 to describe events composed only of real-life actions, without a narrative thread or the use of mimesis. Among the guidelines for happenings were that they were to be given only once in non-theatre spaces and that they should keep fluid the line between performance and life.[25] Closely related to the happenings, and appearing soon after, came experimental works based on the real-life actions of the human body, often called "body art." Like the happenings, body art developed outside the theatre and often, in its presentation of "real" material, in conscious opposition to it. As early as 1913

Marcel Duchamp had shifted attention from the creation of an artistic object out or raw material to selecting an already existing object or experience and presenting it for artistic contemplation. Hence the "ready-mades," and "found" objects, taken from the real world and placed on artistic display. This concept spread in ensuing years from objects of human actions. By the 1960s Bruce Nauman was making videotapes of his body performing natural actions, and many body artists of the 1970s presented real-life actions. Bonnie Sherk performed a piece appropriately named *Sitting Still* in 1970 and later exhibited herself as an actual short-order cook in a pancake house in the 1973 piece *Cleaning the Griddle*. Howard Fried offered audiences the opportunity to view a wrestling match, a baseball game, and a golf lesson as examples of this new form, created only by an imaginary framing of these real-life events.[26]

Clearly the most extreme examples of body art were those that attempted most strongly to remove any traces of the mimetic or the fictional from their presentations, creating pieces that emphasized the physical reality of the body by subjecting it to extreme conditions, even damage. The most famous such work was surely Chris Burden's 1971 *Shoot*, for which a friend actually shot him in the arm with a rifle. The extremity of such actions, Burden explained, was to remove his work completely from theatre, which he dismissed as "bad art." "Getting shot is for real," he explained. "There's no element of pretense or make-believe in it."[27]

Far less extreme examples of the calculated or accidental display of the actor's "real" body go all the way back to classical times, with reports of actors actually dying onstage, actually physically wounded, actually losing control of their emotions or even their sanity. The most extreme examples come from the Roman shows of the late classical period, which varied the straightforward and brutal killing of criminals by wild beasts by staging these killings from time to time as reenactments of mythic stories, so a victim costumed as Icarus might be pushed to his death from a high tower, or a mimic "Orpheus" with only a lyre, exposed to the ravages of real wild bears.[28] Many stories of actors really dying or being wounded come from the middle ages. Undoubtedly many of these reports are what Jody Enders calls "urban legends" in her fascinating study of this phenomenon, *Death by Drama*.[29] Nonetheless, any theatre-goer can recall instances when the "real" body of the actor breaks through the fictive world—it may be so simple a matter as an inadvertent sneeze, or a temporary loss of memory, or it may be as serious as an actual physical injury, but it is an inevitable and even essential part of the total theatre experience.

In more modern, metatheatrical times, such accidents may in fact be part of the action, so that the audience cannot even be sure of their "authenticity." I recall an ill-fated production of *Hedda Gabler* in Greenwich Village in the 1970s, where the maid opened the play by coming onstage and collapsing. So accustomed was the off-off-Broadway audience to metatheatrical tricks in those days that many did not believe that this was not a part of the show until an ambulance arrived to carry off the actress (indeed, a few even then had some suspicions).

Much more clearly conscious are onstage actions that calculatedly call attention to the body, as when the body performs real actions that are not considered "proper" for the current theatrical culture. The rise of "realistic" acting was in large measure a gradual bringing into the theatre bodily actions from the world outside. The great French actor Talma, a major precursor of realism, astonished audiences in the 1821 neoclassical drama *Sylla* by showing them his body lying on a bed. "Never in the whole annals of French tragedy," notes his biographer Collins, "had any hero or heroine gone to bed on stage."[30] The contemporary critic Legouvé actually described step by step how each of the actor's limbs moved to accomplish this action.[31] More recently, other bodily functions have moved from real life onto the stage. In a 2014 production of Molière's *Imaginary Invalid* at the Berlin Volksbühne, the leading Berman actor Martin Wuttke continually hawks and spits, to the delight of the audience (at one point also he receives a huge enema as water spurts from his mouth and ears).

Onstage urination and defecation have been seen on European stages, especially in Germany, for some time, although they remain rare and mostly underground in Anglo-Saxon theatre. The Norwegian experimental artist Vegard Vinge and his company have gained a reputation in Europe with their radical reinterpretations of Ibsen, which always include violent physical action, urination, and defecation, which are clearly not simulated. Such activities, says their leading chronicler in English, Andrew Friedman, "powerfully highlight the live performer laboring beneath the theatrical fantasy."[32]

Although such extremely personal and private demonstrations of the stage figure's bodily reality are a fairly recent theatrical phenomenon, the milder, but originally almost equally shocking stage display of the nude body has been a significant part of the theatre's fascination with the real for the past half-century. Of course, display of the nude or nearly nude female body has long been a feature of burlesque theatres and other venues of marginal reputation, but it was not until the late 1960s that nudity, both male and female, entered the more legitimate theatre, first not surprisingly in more experimental houses, and before the decade ended even in the mainstream theatres of Broadway. Obviously a degree of sexual titillation was normally involved, but more generally such displays reflected both the desire so strong in that turbulent decade to challenge traditional social and cultural mores, and also the continuing project of the modern experimental theatre to break down the barriers between what appeared onstage and offstage life, both public and private. John Houchin, writing on theatre nudity and censorship during the 1960s observes, rather hyperbolically: "The presence of unclad bodies on stage transforms the conventions of theatre into stark reality. There is no longer any illusion or mystery, only a person whose actual physical being is conspicuously present."[33] Certainly, the appearance of a nude body onstage still normally remains a shocking reminder of reality but even in the late 1960s, when the shock value was greater, it hardly dissipated any illusion or mystery, as may be seen in the two best-known examples of stage nudity from that period, the musical *Hair* and Richard Schechner's *Dionysius in '69*, both of which were heavily invested in mystery, illusion, and ritual echoes. And certainly the first male nudity on Broadway, actually only a rear view of Clive Rivell, playing Marat, did nothing to disrupt the powerful theatricality of Peter Brook's *Marat/Sade* in 1965. One might assume that as stage nudity has, like all previous intrusions of the "real" onstage become more and more common, its shock value has diminished and with it, its reminding the audience of the real body beneath the stage figure. A notorious German production of 2013 clearly refutes this assumption, however. In his highly political contemporary staging of Verdi's *Ballo in Maschera*, set in the smoldering ruins of the World Trade Center, Kresnik utilized thirty-five nude extras, wearing only Mickey Mouse masks, to stand for the wretched victims of late capitalism. These were not actors, but actually pensioners, whose elderly, sagging bodies, in distinct contrast to the tradition of attractive stage nudity, brought just the shock of the real that suited Kresnik's political message.

The display of the working, suffering, or unclad body has thus for the last half century provided an important repository of the "real" onstage. Although such displays have generally either been called for in the script (as in *Dionysius in '69*) or imposed by the director (as in Kresnik's *Ballo in Maschera*), this "real" is the physical reality of the actor's body, not of the actor as an individual human being with an extra-theatrical life, as was the case for example of Buffalo Bill Cody. Early in the 1970s a number of female performance artists began turning away from the male-dominated body art of the previous decade to emphasize a different experience of the real, one that was embedded in a social and cultural context. The dancer Yvonne Rainer, one of the leaders in this shift, reported in 1973 that she was "involved with finding ways to use performers as something other than demonstrators of behavioral and kinetic phenomena."[34] As Eleanor Antin, herself a leading performance artist, observed in 1978, feminist performance of that decade was much less concerned with abstractions than with the specific and "very real political questions" about "what it means to be a woman in this society, a particular woman, an artist."[35] This, of course, very frequently resulted in performances that specifically recounted events in the performer's personal history, celebrating the positive and self-empowering, exorcising or seeking social redress or sympathetic understanding for the negative and self-diminishing. Autobiographical performance not only provided a position from which a performer could explore, express, and even perhaps seek her own identity, it also provided a forum in which she could reach out to other women whose experiences might parallel her own.

These works by female performance artists in turn served as

models for performers of various ethnic and sexual minorities who had found that the traditional white, male-dominated, heterosexual theatre provided little space for the articulation of their experience or concerns, autobiographical performance offered to them an important venue for this articulation. The range of such performance steadily expanded and soon moved beyond the domain of performance art into mainstream theatre as well.

As autobiographical performance increased in popularity and visibility, however, its truth claims, so important in the 1970s, came increasingly under suspicion. Even when working with their own autobiography, performers began to realize they were not presenting an uncompromised, pure self, but a self-constructed according to certain codes. Some such codes operated on the level of the organization of material—codes of selection, of narration, of representation, of performance (the same recognition, as I have noted, was undermining the truth claims of documentary theatre at this same time). Perhaps even more importantly, especially after the revolutionary new perspective on gender as performance offered by Judith Butler in 1990, was the recognition of the operation of other often unrecognized codes governing gender, sexuality, and all sorts of human behavior. In short, the real-life "identity" articulated by autobiographical performance was discovered to be already a role, a character, following scripts not controlled by the performer, but by the culture as a whole.

This recognition did not diminish the importance of autobiographical performance, nor of the widespread use of autobiographical material by performance artists concerned with the exploration of questions of identity, particularly in relation to social and political questions any more than it diminished an interest in the documentary drama. What has happened, however, is that a good deal of such work has become much more self-reflexive, much more aware of its own constructedness, and much more willing to make this awareness itself part of the presentation. Thus, gay performance artist Tim Miller's 1991 *Sex/Love/Stories* revealingly opened with Miller's observation: "I remember so many things; some of them even happened."[36] Spalding Gray's 1990 stage monologue (his thirteenth), *Monster in a Box*, was a series of reflections precisely about the process of gathering and arranging the material for one of his works. When recent stage monologists like Gray present accounts of their visits to doctors or trips abroad, these events, even though actually experienced, were clearly experienced with the idea that they would subsequently be reworked for stage narratives. It is, on a much more domestic plane, the same feedback loop between life and theatre practiced by Buffalo Bill in theatres a century earlier.

This shift from the stage appearance of real-life celebrities like Buffalo Bill or Frank James to the stage appearance of more everyday people like Eleanor Antin or Tim Miller not only reflected a change in orientation of solo performance, but in the more conventional theatrical practice of involving a number of performers, where the "real" being introduced is less autobiographical than social or cultural, as may be seen in Kresnik's nude chorus. The center of such work in the late twentieth and early twenty-first centuries has been Germany, although important examples have appeared elsewhere as well. Most theatre scholars would agree that the leading contemporary company involved in this new wave of bringing real material, especially human material, onto the stage has been the German group Rimini Protokoll. The group was formed in 1999 and since then has been the leader in a new approach toward mixing theatre and the "real" world. Rimini Protokoll generally uses performers who are not professional actors, but the group avoids the use of the word *amateur*. The participants in these productions are rather "experts," but "experts of the everyday," and onstage they present material from their area of expertise, which is their own life experience. Of their work the journal *Frankfurter Rundshau* reported: "Rimini Protokoll brings real life to the stage in a way that no other theatre form has been able to. The unmistakable strength of these performances lies above all in the fact that in spite of the proximity to the persons whom they portray a rift appears between the role and the personality, and with it an awareness of the risk that life could gain the upper hand, and theatre could lose control over itself."[37] For many of their productions, Rimini Protokoll has sought for participants whose own personal stories can be woven into a coherent performance text. Thus, for example, in their 2012 *Radio Muzzein*, three of the men who call for prayers from minaret towers in Cairo talked of their everyday life, their beliefs, and their concern about the fact that their age-old profession is being replaced by electronic recordings. Rarely has Rimini Proto-koll worked with a traditional dramatic text, but their 2007 *Wallenstein*, one of their most innovative and praised creations, in fact ingeniously used Schiller's play as a framework for mixing fiction and reality. They selected persons who in various ways suggested Schiller's major characters—a Weimar politician whose party had turned against him, an astrologer, a woman who ran a dating service to arrange extramarital affairs, Vietnam veterans, and so on, weaving them and their actual life stories into a structure governed by the events of Schiller's plot.

The success of Rimini Protokoll launched a new wave of German use not only of bodies, but of personae brought in from the real world, and many of the leading new experimental groups of the new century there experimented with such material. She She Pop, a feminist performance collective organized the same year at the same experimental university (Giessen) as Rimini Protokoll, in their best known piece, *Testament* (2011), brought the fathers of company members onstage to help present a meditation on *King Lear* and to discuss generation tensions and the processes of theatre. Gob Squad, a British-German collection formed in 1994, have specialized in audience involvement and mixed-media per-formances, but they too have recently turned toward nonactors, most notably in *Before Your Very Eyes*, invited to the prestigious Berlin Theatertreffen in 2011. Here the audience, seated behind a one-way mirror, watched a group of eight- to fourteen-year-old children first playing extemporaneously in a colorful play room, then encouraged by instructions from a loudspeaker to create sketches and improvisations about adult life.

Neither Rimini Protokoll nor its most important sister groups have used real bodies to make specific political points, but given the modern German tradition of political commentary in the the-atre, a number of important directors have done so. Kresnik has already been mentioned, but probably the director most associ-ated with such work is Volker Lösch. In a culture of controversial directors, the *Guardian* suggested in 2013 that he might be the "most controversial."[38] Lösch's approach is firmly within the new reality onstage tradition, but he has particularly employed one central device, creating a chorus of nonactors who in some way reflected a basic concern of the production. Thus his production of Wedekind's *Lulu* (2010) utilized a chorus of actual Berlin sex workers, his production of Alfred Döblin's *Berlin Alexanderplatz* had a chorus that emerged from the audiences and identified themselves as convicted criminals and felons, while homeless people from the streets of Hamburg provided the chorus for his 2011 *Marat/Sade*. Unlike the nude pensioners in Kresnik's *Ballo in Maschera*, who served only as a visual symbol of the negative effects of late capitalism, each of these choruses were extensively interviewed by Lösch, and material from these interviews was worked into the stage text and recited by the chorus. Such direct representations of contemporary social reality have aroused continual controversy, and sometimes legal challenges, as when the chorus in *Marat/Sade*, in a further blurring of theatre and reality, ended the production by citing the names, incomes, and addresses of Hamburg's wealthiest citizens, among the wealthiest in Germany and the world.[39]

As these recent examples remind us, the bringing of "real" material onto the stage, whether it be the real bodies or actors or real current social issues, has always potentially carried with it not only an aesthetic challenge but often a social and cultural one as well. A wide variety of forces have historically opposed such activity, some on aesthetic grounds, that the purity of the art was being threatened, some on grounds of morality and taste (from Talma lying down on a bed to nude bodies, to real sex workers or convicts) and some on political grounds (the revelation of material, documentary or visual, that certain members of society do not want so publicly revealed). The situation is especially complicated in the case of nonactors. Lösch and Kresnik have been accused not only of sensationalism but of exploitation in their use of real human material, however consensual that use has been. Such tensions clearly will continue to mark the ongoing use of real bodies and real persona, a major part of modern European theatre.

A particularly striking recent case indicates the complexities—aesthetic, social, and moral—of this growing practice in contemporary theatre. This is the *Disabled Theatre* of French choreographer Jerôme Bel, which has stirred heated discussion internationally since its premiere in 2013. From the beginning of his career, Bel has been very much involved with the use of nondance material in his work—indeed, in France he is generally regarded as the leader of what is called the "nondance" movement. Bel has, from the beginning of his career, been much closer to the experimental performance work discussed above than to conventional dance. His first piece, the 1994 *Nom donné par l'auteur*, resembled a happening more than a dance, with two seated performers facing each other and manipulating objects like a vacuum clear and a hair dryer. His next work, *Jerôme Bel* (1995), involved four naked performers and onstage urination. Nondancers performing ordinary movements are common in his work, and he has even presented autobiographical works, such as *Véronique Doisneau* (2004), primarily a monologue by that dancer recalling her career as a minor chorus member in the French opera. In 2013 Bel was approached by the theatre HORA of Zurich, a producing organization founded in 1993 for people with learning disabilities, primarily Down syndrome. Over the years they have worked with a series of guest directors and choreographers, but Bel created with them something new and much closer to his own interests. In the first part of the work he created with HORA, each actor introduced him or herself to the audience, in the second part, each performed a dance sequence choreographed by themselves, and in the final section each spoke of their experience in creating this work. The production was both tremendously moving and profoundly disturbing, as it was clearly meant to be, constantly testing the boundaries not only between life and dance, but between how audiences are to react to a display that hovers somewhere between exploitation and expressive fulfillment, between shock and empathy, between aversion and fascination. The power of the real to disrupt all conventional assumptions about the arts of theatre and dance was surely never more effectively displayed than in this remarkable piece.

CHAPTER 3

There Must Be a Lot of Fish in That Lake

Although the body of the actor and the words he or she uses are in almost every theatre culture appropriated fairly directly from experience outside the theatre and thus are always susceptible to some "bleeding through" of their nontheatrical reality, the same cannot really be said for the general physical surroundings of the actor. The normal image of a theatrical performance is one that takes place inside a space particularly created for such activity. Thus, although the actor and his or her language come in from outside, the space within which he performs is most often constructed as part of the theatre apparatus, even when it imitates extra-theatrical spaces. The Western theatre, from the ancient Greeks until the move toward realism at the end of the eighteenth century, usually used fairly neutral backgrounds, predominantly composed of architectural elements, in front of which the actors performed. A similar neutrality is found in other major theatrical traditions, most famously in the Japanese Noh, with its invariable stylized background and its single pine tree.

One can surely say that in all theatrical cultures which have developed a performance space set apart from the normal world of human activity, that space has served as a kind of site of imagination, subject to certain rules, a fundamental one being that the audience agrees to serve as spectators and accept as "real" the fictive world being presented to them by the actors. The performance space itself thus serves as a kind of "frame," emphasizing this dynamic (indeed, an alternative name from the proscenium-arch theatre is the "picture-frame stage" and some late-nineteenth-century British theatres in fact surrounded the stage on all four sides with an ornate frame). Traditionally, this performance space, the stage and auditorium, is not entered directly from the outside world, but is separated from that world by a liminal area, as a kind of mimetic air-lock, the theatre lobby, which allows audiences to move by stages into the particular illusory realm of the theatre.

Theatrical performances that were not "protected" by this house of illusion have been much more susceptible, as we shall see, to incursions from the physical world. Even the classical Greek stage, forming a partial enclosure, could and apparently did take advantage of the major "real world" accessible to its audiences, including the open sky above them. Thus, many of the extant plays, among them *Oedipus* and *Antigone* begin at or near dawn, and it is difficult to image that the plays, which were presented at that hour, did not take advantage of this contribution from the real world. Performances outside theatrical structures are naturally much more open to such effects, as can be seen in the two periods in Western theatre when there was extensive such activity—the medieval period, before the creation of modern theatre structures—and from the end of the nineteenth century onward, when, often in the search of more "reality," productions outside conventional theatre structures became increasingly common.

The phenomenologist Bert O. States pointed out that one of the central features, and indeed a source of particular power in the theatre, as that so many of the objects encountered there are "pieces of reality," to which extra artistic meanings have been given.[1] Thus a real chair in most productions today would be used to represent a chair in Hedda Gabler's living room (I will talk more about such objects in the following chapter). In semiotic terms, the chair would be an icon, a sign that is in some way like the thing it stands for. The classic semiotic term does not distinguish between an actual chair or a chair painted on the wall of a set, very common in the eighteenth century. Thus Keir Elam, author of the first modern book on theatre semiotics in English, suggested that a further term be used for an actual chair representing a chair in a play, "iconic identity."[2] Iconic identity, although quite common, especially in the modern, realistic theatre, and especially in items of furnishing and decoration, or in hand properties, has traditionally almost never extended to the setting, the actual physical surroundings of the actors. A chair onstage will normally actually be represented by a chair, but a tree or a house will be painted or built for the occasion. Medieval open-air religious festivals, however, suggest another possibility, which would be much more extensively developed in modern times.

In the very earliest liturgical dramas of the Middle Ages, we find already a complex mixture of mimesis and reality. When the tenth-century *Quem Quaeritis* trope began to be performed as a dramatic text, the three Marys were impersonated by young men, generally assumed to be standing before the main altar of the church.[3] As liturgical drama became more elaborate, other parts of the cathedral were used, but although these were "real" locations, they were presumably accepted as suitable symbolically, reinforcing the effect of the performance on a symbolic, if not on a realistic level. When religious dramas began to be performed outside the cathedrals, the utilization of the physical surroundings became much more complex. Often these plays remained in the vicinity of the cathedral, particularly on its wide front platform and steps, and the cathedral provided not merely a rich decorative background, like the classical Roman stage, but appeared in its "true" role as the abode of God and the angelic choirs, as may be seen in the famous medieval play, the twelfth-century Anglo-Norman *Jeu d'Adam*.[4] In some cases this "theatricalization" of real places could involve a large part of the city, most notably in the passion processionals that are still echoed in the widespread via dolorosa process of modern times. As early as the fifteenth century, Vienna staged the public humiliation of Christ in the city marketplace, and then the actor bore his cross through the winding streets of the city to the distant cemetery where the crucifixion and resurrection were to be enacted. The market, the streets, the cemetery, and even the watching public, were thus elements of the real world imaginatively refigured as parts of the universal city, Jerusalem.[5] There is still of course a certain slippage between the Vienna cemetery and what it represents, because although it is a *real* cemetery, it is not the site it imaginatively represents. This distinction is of particular importance in reference to sacred sites, which inevitably take on some aura of the actions that reportedly occurred there.

In fact, the most ancient records that we have of theatrical activity are ritual observances carried out in specific sacred locations, which are essential to the event. The ancient Egyptian texts from Abydos, whose "passion play" of Osiris is often cited as the earliest known theatrical text, was performed annually for some two thousand years, beginning in the second millennia BCE. These texts were presented at the most sacred site in Egypt, the island where Osiris was reported buried.[6] Jerusalem also witnessed theatrical activities at its major sites from very early times, as may be seen in the first detailed reports that we have from a pilgrim to that city, Egeria in 381–84. She reports a number of commemorative activities at various sacred sites, including a reenactment of the triumphal entry of Palm Sunday with "the bishop led in the same manner as the Lord once was led," accompanied by children singing hosannas and waving palm and olive branches.[7]

In more modern times reenactments of significant past events have become increasingly common, although today, the great majority of them are concerned with historic or secular subjects, not religious ones. There are important exceptions, however, such as the Hill Cumorah Pageant in upstate New York, a major dramatic spectacle that traces the history of the Mormon Church and takes place on the hill where, according to the Mormon faith, Joseph Smith, directed by the angel Moroni, discovered the golden tablets establishing that faith.

Although the most productive years of medieval drama, in the fourteenth and fifteenth centuries, saw a continuation of outdoor productions, theatre producers were not inspired by this circumstance to utilize natural settings for their productions. On the contrary, for the most part, their actors performed in front of usually rather booth-like structures called "mansions," or, in England and Spain, on individual wagons with apparently only modest scenic background that was essentially artificial.

With the Renaissance, and the theatre moving indoors, the concept of the actor performing in any sort of "real" surrounding was almost completely lost. Even when the great baroque festivals moved out of doors, as Louis XIV's famous *Pleasures of the*

Enchanted Island, performances either occurred within a court-
yard whose classical architectural background was a neutral as a
Roman stage façade, or in the royal park, where natural elements
like trees and water were subjected to such ruthless control that
every possible trace of the natural had been removed. Rather than
stress the "naturalness" of nature, as the romantics would strive
to do later, classical and baroque designers sought to create what
landscape historian Elizabeth Barlow Rodgers calls "theatrical ar-
rangements of landscape." Not only were natural elements made
theatrical, Rodgers further notes, but "many of the gardens of this
period contained actual outdoor theatres with a grassy stage,
hedges for wings, and sometimes, peeping forth from the green-
ery, terra-cotta figures representing stock characters from the
commedia dell'arte" (emphasis in the original).[8]

A remarkable early example of an almost opposite aesthetic,
and one much closer to modern experimentation, was undertaken
by Goethe in 1782, early in his Weimar years. Goethe invited
members of the Weimar court to an evening entertainment he
had devised himself, a small comic opera called *The Fishermen.*
They assembled at a small pavilion in the court park appropriately called *"the Cottage of the Muses."* Entering the small building, they found seats arranged facing the back wall of the cottage,
which had been removed to provide a frame for the actual landscape outside, a wooded glade and the bend of a stream. The audience was reportedly entranced by the sight of a real boat moved
down the real stream by a singing oarsman and by the mysterious
effect of lanterns carried by actors bobbing in amongst the trees.[9]

It would not be an exaggeration to say that this modest court
entertainment represented the most fully realized theatrical representation to date of what would come to be recognized as the
romantic aesthetic—the emphasis upon nature and the natural,
upon rustic simplicity, upon the sort of atmosphere created by
lanterns and moonlight. All this was much in tone with a changing aesthetic in Europe. At this same time in London, landscape
designer Philip James de Loutherbourg was creating a revolution
in British scenic design by creating artificially on David Garrick's
stage just the sort of visual world Goethe was presenting in reality in Weimar, while the year after Goethe's production, 1783,
Marie Antoinette established at Versailles her Petit Hameau, a

theatrical rustic retreat where she and her courtiers could play at being peasants amid a bucolic setting with real cows. There is a distinct difference of course between the real rural setting displayed by Goethe, the imitative but habitable rural setting created for Marie Antoinette, and the stage imitations of such settings designed by de Loutherbourg, but all shared to same desire to make contact with the "real" and all sought this in the somewhat mysterious realm of nature so beloved by the romantic imagination. Much of the later history of the attraction of scenic design to extra-theatrical reality can be traced back to this romantic vision and to these late eighteenth century experiments.

No one articulated more clearly than Victor Hugo the bond between nature and the real and the centrality of the real to romantic art in general and the theatre in particular. In his best-known statement on this subject, the 1827 *Preface to Cromwell*, he asserts that "the poetry of our time" is the drama, and "the characteristic of the drama is the real." He continues, "In the drama, as it may be conceived at least, if not executed, all the parts cohere and everything happens as in real life." Even though one may protest, with justification, that this hardly applies to the larger-than-life heroes and melodramatic turns of a Hugo drama, it marks out a direction that the future realistic drama, in many ways an outgrowth of romanticism, would follow. In the present context, Hugo's remarks on reality and scenic design are particularly important: "We are beginning to realize in our day," he observes

> that exactness in the matter of locality is one of the most essential elements of reality. The speaking or acting characters are not the only ones who leave a faithful impression upon the mind of the spectator. The place where this or that catastrophe occurred becomes an incorruptible and convincing witness to it; and the absence of this sort of silent character makes the grandest scenes of history incomplete upon the stage. What poet would dare murder Rizzio elsewhere than in Mary Stuart's chamber? To stab Henri IV elsewhere than in the Rue de la Ferronerie, blocked up with drays and carriages?
>
> To burn Jeanne d'Arc elsewhere than in the Old Marketplace?[10]

For a modern reader, this may well seem a call for the development of what would later come to be called site-specific theatre, and indeed it may be considered as helping prepare the way intellectually for such work, but for Hugo and his contemporaries the implications of this passage were not that radical, though radical enough. He was calling for theatre settings to reflect iconically their presumed locations, differing from play to play and even, it might be, from scene to scene, rather than relying upon the single neutral antechambers used for Racine and the tradition he represented.

For most of the following century the romantics and the realists who followed them worked in this direction, creating scenic designs that reflected with greater and greater realistic accuracy the locations indicated in the dramatic text. Shakespeare, the dramatist most favored by the romantics, also presented the greatest challenge to this approach. The English director Charles Kean was honored for both the splendor of his Shakespearian productions and for their historical accuracy. As the Duke of Newcastle reported: "there is nothing which he introduces upon the stage for which he has not authority, and you may see the living representations of Shakespeare's characters, with the exact costume, the exact scenery."[11] Scrupulous historical accuracy came to be expected later in the century, even though this required elaborate and expensive machinery such as turntables, sliding, and elevator stages in order to provide realistic representations of Shakespeare's multi-scene dramatic worlds. The culmination of this monumental approach to visual realism in Shakespeare came at the end of the century in the productions of English directors Henry Irving and Herbert Beerbohm Tree, although its limits were also suggested by perhaps the most famous production of this type, Beerbohm Tree's 1911 revival of *A Midsummer Night's Dream* with live rabbits and a mossy stage floor sprouting live flowers that could be plucked by the actors.

Nor was Shakespeare unique in this late-nineteenth-century passion for "real" stage environments. The lavish historical spectacles that Sardou created for Sarah Bernhardt in France featured similar visual extravagance, carefully researched down to the last detail, such as the colors of glass available in the Byzantine court of the epic *Theodora*, which incidentally also included live lions and tigers.[12] The same tendency could also be seen in the much more modest depictions of everyday life that also grew in popularity from midcentury on. Early in the nineteenth century, the traditional system of representing domestic rooms by painted side wings and a flat backdrop, often with two-dimensional furniture painted on them, began to be replaced by the modern box set, much closer in appearance to a real room, with real doors and doorknobs, real molding, and three-dimensional furniture. The director primarily associated with change was Mme. Vestris in the 1820s and 1830s, who brought to these humbler scenic environments a similar search for realism that Kean brought to Shakespeare in the following decade. An 1833 review notes that her stage's "more perfect enclosure gives the appearance of a private chamber, infinitely better than the old contrivance of wings."[13]

Like monumental realistic Shakespeare, such domestic illusions of everyday life reached their apotheosis at the turn of the next century—in this case, in the work of David Belasco, perhaps the most famous champion of realism in scenic environments. For one production, *The Easiest Way* (1909), Belasco purchased the furnishings, lighting devices, even the wall coverings from a tenement in New York's Tenderloin district and created an on-stage replica from them.[14] His production of *The Governor's Lady* (1912) received thunderous applause for its detailed recreation of one of the then-popular chain of New York restaurants, Child's, in which the audience could even smell the coffee and pancakes being prepared. Again, Belasco obtained actual elements from the Restaurant Company, and created so complete an image that, according to *Theatre Magazine*: "It is as if he had taken the audience during the intermission, walked them around the corner of Seventh Avenue and seated them to one side of the Child's restaurant at that location and let the last act be played there."[15] Belasco himself boasted that he purposely blurred the boundaries of the real and the fictional, seeking to make his audience "forget that it is not looking into a real place." A proper stage setting, he said, should transport audiences out of their seats and into the fictional world onstage.[16] This image, and the similar one from *Theatre Magazine*, anticipate, of course, certain experiments of the twentieth century, such as promenade and immersive productions, which would do exactly that.

The rise of the cinema, which could bring these actual locations into the film house, largely ended this stage tradition, but enough appeal remained in the bringing of such real items and effects on that that from time to time during the next century, productions achieved considerable success drawing upon the old Belasco model. This was particularly true in the post–Depression 1930s, when the theatre sought to attract audiences both with elaborate visual effects and dramas dealing with social inequality. One of the most successful plays in New York, *Tobacco Road* (1933), revived the Belasco approach in almost every detail, with comparable success. The designer, Sharpe, revived a flagging career with his stunning recreation of a Georgia sharecropper's squalid yard and shack. Tons of real dirt covered the stage floor and Sharpe combed junkyards and vacant lots for rusty cans, corncobs, and inner tubes. Instead of designing costumes, he asked a cast member who owned a farm in South Carolina to call her caretaker and buy worn-out pants, shirts, and dresses from the poorest of the hired workers there. Even though the play received mixed reviews, the setting dazzled audiences and critics alike. The *Time Magazine* critic reported that "the small of hot dust, of unwashed bedding and dried food leavings seems to drift out over Manhattan audiences."[17] Just two years later, appropriately enough at the Belasco Theatre, New York's leading designer Norman Bel Geddes took advantage of the huge and deep stage Belasco created to outdo the master with his setting for Sidney Kingsley's *Dead End*, showing the back of an elegant apartment building overlooking wharf-side tenements strewn with junk and laundry. The orchestra pit, filled with water, represented the East River, where a teenage gang dove and splashed. *New York Times* critic Brooks Atkinson noted that Bel Geddes had "filled the stage with one of those super-realistic settings that David Belasco liked to contrive, solid down to the ring of shoes on asphalt pavement."

Even during the period of the greatest vogue for spectacularly detailed scenic environments on stage, the era of Irving, Beerbohm Tree, and Belasco, the theatrical fascination with real settings began to develop in a completely different direction, following the somewhat whimsical comment of the *Theatre Magazine* reviewer of Belasco's *Governor's Lady*, that it was as if Belasco had led the audience out of the theatre and around the corner into a real Child's restaurant. An early example of such activity was undertaken by an amateur society in England, the Pastoral Players, which caused a stir in artistic circles in the mid-1880s with their outdoor productions of pastoral plays by Shakespeare and Fletcher in the Coombe Wood in South London. Typical was the glowing report in *Era* magazine: "Not only did he mounting leave nothing to the imagination, more even than imitating reality with photographic accuracy, it was reality itself."[18] Another journal suggested that such surroundings were far better than conventional stages not only for the audiences but also for the actors:

> Instead of facing thin edges of canvas and carpentry at the wings, they are looking at realities, real rounded tress, living grass, glades and prospect. Their scene is as good as that present to the audience. There is no sham. The sun is really shining for them, the birds are singing, the leaves and blades of grass and flowers really waving in the breeze.[19]

In the opening years of the twentieth century, open-air theatres, offering "reality itself" enjoyed a great vogue among summer tourists in both Europe and America. Probably the most famous of these was the first of many modern outdoor theatres in Germany, the Harzer Bergtheater, founded in 1903 by nationalist Ernst Wachler as a "people's theatre" free from the contamination of traditional theatre culture. Although Wachler favored work drawn from Teutonic myth, his most successful offering was *A Midsummer Night's Dream*, in 1914.

A closely related phenomenon was the "Pageant Movement," launched by a celebration in Sherborne, England, in 1905. To celebrate the 1200th anniversary of the town's founding in 705, a locally born playwright, Louis Napoleon Parker, inspired by medieval mystery plays, the Wagner Festival, Oberammergau, and the recent Bergtheater and William Tell performances in Altdorf, Germany, created a dramatized history and allegory of Sherborne set in the ruins of a twelfth-century castle and utilizing over 900 performers.[20] The success of this event, fueled by local pride, patriotism, and a deluge of tourists, inspired a vogue of pageants, first in England, and shortly thereafter in the United States, almost all dealing with local history and not a few in specific locations associated with that history. In 1913 the American Pageant Association listed forty-six such celebrations in fifteen states, and the vogue continued until well into the 1930s. Frank Lascalles, known as "the man who staged the Empire," was the most prominent creator of such spectacles. He trained, appropriately enough, as an actor with Beerbohm Tree, and went on to stage historical pageants first in England and eventually in Quebec, South Africa, and Calcutta.[21] Historical re-creations in real or simulated environments were central to all of these. The London Festival of 1910 (involving over 15,000 participants) was set within and on the grounds of the Crystal Palace, but still this environmental tradition was maintained for such scenes as the Danish invasions. "The river up which the Vikings sailed cannot be brought to the Crystal Palace," noted the *Los Angeles Times* regretfully, "but the lakes in the grounds will be utilized and spectators will witness London bridge break in the middle and the defenders hurled into the water."[22]

Surely the most influential director internationally in the early twentieth century was Germany's Max Reinhardt, whose eclectic body of work contributed significantly to almost every style of theatrical production of his era. When Reinhardt began his career at the opening of the twentieth century, the fashionable style was detailed realism of the Belasco and Beerbohm Tree variety, represented in Berlin by the work of Otto Brahm, where J. L. Styan reports: "Every prop or piece of furniture on stage had to be as authentic as possible, and every detail of speech or movement, however small, had to be perfected to the point where an audience was convinced it was seeing the real thing."[23]

Reinhardt's first major success, his 1905 *Midsummer Night's Dream*, did not abandon the ideal of the real, but introduced a more poetic, impressionist tone, his forest not composed of entire trees but a maze of tangled trunks that stretched upward out of sight. These, insisted Hugo von Hofmannthal, who adapted the Shakespearian text: "more nearly approximated reality," adding that the forest floor "was made of a firm carpet of tall grass" in which the lovers "lay as naturally as young people do in a field that they have found on a day in the country."[24] In later versions of this play, Reinhardt moved away from such realism while in the theatre, but in 1932 he followed the example of the Pastoral Players by creating an outdoor production on the ground of his elegant residence, the Schloss Leopoldskron in Salzburg. The following year he offered outdoor productions in Florence and most notably in Oxford, where in a great open meadow, he was able to think in terms "not of square feet but of acres,"[25] with powerful use of distant perspectives and lantern scene as night fell.

Although Reinhardt's theatricalization of real space was only part of his wide-ranging experimentation, it was profoundly influential on later site-specific theatre. This work was launched with one of his most famous productions, von Hofmannsthal's *Everyman*, which inaugurated the Salzburg Festival in 1920. Here, taking inspiration from the open-air productions of the medieval period, Reinhardt placed the action on a large platform set before the doors of the Salzburg Cathedral, and the entire area was incorporated into the performance, with characters entering from side streets and bells rung or cries shouted at appropriate moments from towers elsewhere in the city. Even nature was theatricalized, as Hofmannsthal reports:

> One of these criers had been placed in the highest tower of a medieval castle, built far above the city, and his voice sounded, weird and ghostly, about five seconds after the others, just as the first rays of the rising moon fell cold and strange from the high heavens on the hearts of the audience.[26]

The Salzburg Festival inspired some of Reinhardt's most ambitious open-air productions. In 1933 Reinhardt's designer Clemens Holzmeister built an entire small medieval village with trees, bushes, and flowers that grew from summer to summer as the production was revived. Once again, nature was pressed into theatrical service: "moon and stars joined in the play, and gusts of the night wind led from a sultry evening to the pallid dawn of the dungeon scene."[27] The following year, Reinhardt produced one of his most striking and influential outdoor productions, *The Merchant of Venice* actually staged in a small square in Venice in front of a palazzo that Reinhardt claimed had actually been the resident of a Jewish merchant in Shakespearian times and with a bridge at the rear over a small canal, along which gondolas passed to and fro and upon which the elegant Spanish barque of the Prince of Aragon arrived with its noble suitor.[28]

Reinhardt's productions in found locations of this type inspired a number of directors in Germany and Italy, where a several Goldoni plays were presented in appropriate town squares, but not really in England, where, despite the Pageant Players and a strong tradition of amateur open-air festivals, no major professional theatre or director explored this approach until 1937. The impetus then came from outside the country and the theatre establishment. The Danish Tourist Board, seeking some major festival event to mark the Silver Jubilee of King Christian X, invited the then-leading British Shakespearian theatre, the Old Vic, to present a festival production of *Hamlet* at Elsinore Castle, its presumed actual location (although the current castle was built in the sixteenth century, contemporary with Shakespeare, but centuries after the historical Hamlet, if he indeed really existed). Thus, in June 1937, the Old Vic Company, headed by Laurence Olivier and Vivien Leigh and directed by Tyrone Guthrie, went to perform *Hamlet*, "in his own home" or "in its rightful setting" as the British press announced it.[29] In fact, opening night had to be moved to an improvised local hall and the "rightful setting" was not achieved until the second evening.

Robert Shaughnessy, who provides an excellent account of this project and its motivations, characterizes it as "a site-specific event exploiting the convergence between the cultural authority of the play and the magic of this 'authentic' location."[30] His description (including the scare quotes around *authentic*) is quite sound, but his use of the term *site-specific*, needs examination, especially as it will play a central role later in this chapter. No one associated with the 1937 Elsinore production would have used this term, which did not enter the theatrical vocabulary until the early 1980s. I will discuss that term more fully in that context, but the Elsinore project does seem to anticipate such performance, being a production that is designed to be presented in a certain, almost invariably nontheatrical location.

Looking not forward, but a century backward, we seem, at least at first glance, to have in such productions as the Elsinore *Hamlet* or the Venetian *Merchant of Venice* literal fulfillments of Victor Hugo's vision of a performance in its correct historical location, where the walls themselves bore silent witness to the event. Indeed, almost exactly this thought was expressed by the London *Times* of June 4, 1937: "The ghost not only of Hamlet's father but of all the vast and shadowy legend of the Danish Prince haunts the green roofs, the fantastic pinnacles, the dungeons, the great embattled strength of Elsinore."[31] The problem with this vision of course is not only that Hamlet, if he ever existed, never witnessed any of this architecture, or vice versa, but more importantly, the "real world" being evoked here is not as in Hugo, drawn from historical events, but from a dramatic fiction, as was the Reinhardt *Merchant*, however authentic its Renaissance palazzos and gondolas.

To find a theatrical experiment that in fact seems to fulfill Hugo's vision of the ideal historical setting, we must look elsewhere, not to the various location-specific Shakespearian experiments but to the "new pageant" tradition, already mentioned, and to the closely related tradition of historical reenactments of specific events, primarily battles, already referred to in the previous chapter. Although in fact recorded as early as the seventeenth century, quasi-theatrical events of this kind became extremely popular in the late nineteenth and early twentieth centuries. The most famous and spectacular of these was *The Storming of the Winter Palace* on November 7, 1920, a dramatic reenactment of that major event of the Russian Revolution, involving over 8,000 participants, tanks, armored vehicles, even the battleship *Aurora*. The director, Nikolai Evreinov, essentially echoed Hugo by stressing the fact that this work was "performed in the *actual place* where the historic event occurred."[32] Although such reenactments were fairly common in the early twentieth century, often as part of the pageant movement, both gradually faded away before the beginning of the Second World War. Their main remnants during the rest of the century were the historical outdoor pageants, especially those created by Paul Green, a form that he called "symphonic drama."

Like the pageants, the symphonic dramas were largely amateur productions, created at specific locations and depicting the story of those locations. Originally designed, like the pageants, to raise awareness of local history and stimulate civic pride in a largely local audience, the symphonic dramas, a number of which are still annually presented, soon became tourist attractions and came to rely upon a visiting audience. The first such production, in 1923, was the *Ramona Pageant* in Hemet, California, based not on actual historical events, but on a popular historical novel set in this region in the late 1800s and telling of the star-crossed lovers Ramona and her Indian lover Alessandro. Even before the creation of this play, tourists flocked to the area to visit the so-called House of Ramona or Ramona's Marriage Place, just as one can today visit the so-called Home of Juliet in Verona, Italy. The production was set in a natural amphitheater, a small canyon with Indian huts dotting the hillsides and Ramona's adobe hacienda as the main scenic element. The production is still presented today and has been designated California's official outdoor pageant.[33]

Most such productions were however based on actual events and presented in the historic location of these events. After the *Ramona Pageant*, Paul Green, hitherto a successful author of conventional drama, turned to this form and soon dominated it, beginning with *The Lost Colony* in 1937, performed on the site of the colony on Roanoke Island, Virginia, founded by Sir Walter Raleigh in the 1580s. For more than thirty years, until the late 1960s, Green created a series of such dramas, often on commission from particular states, among them Florida, Kentucky, and Ohio, to commemorate key events in the history of those states. Many of these continue to be performed, although *Cross and Sword*, created in 1965 in Saint Augustine to present the early history of that city and later named Florida's state play, ceased presentations in 1996.

Except for the symphonic dramas, the pageant movement never really revived, but the reenactments of historic battles enjoyed a major revival in the United States in the 1960s, for the centennial of the Civil War, and again in the 1970s for the bicentennial of the American Revolution. Countless battles and other historical events were re-created in their original locations with participants in authentic costume attempting to follow with varying exactness the events of a century or two before. This activity—part hobby, part recreation—has spread over the United States, then to Britain, and today is found around the world.

Another popular form of the theatricalization of physical locations, and even more closely tied to actual physical sites were the sound and light shows of the late twentieth century, a type of outdoor entertainment credited to Paul Robert-Housin, who offered a sound and light show at the Château de Chambord in 1952. Normally no actors are involved in such productions, but audiences are seated out of doors within sight of some important historic location, normally a building, while the story of that building is presented by recorded voices and music, heightened by lighting effects. Here may be seen the purest example of the theatricalization of a specific real physical setting. A voice has at last been given to Hugo's hitherto "silent witness" of great historical events. France has been a particular center of such events, but they are now a worldwide activity, with examples across Europe, in the Americas, in Egypt and Israel, in Australia and India. Many of the world's great tourist sites have received this theatrical enhancement, among them the Pyramids of Giza, the Roman Forum, and the Parthenon.

Despite their considerable social and cultural importance, neither the pageant movement nor historical reenactments (with a few exceptions) have attracted much attention from theatre historians, and standard histories of the theatre tend to ignore both, as civic festivals or leisure-time activities. Nevertheless, the sort of blending of fiction, history, and real locations in fact had very close ties however to a movement that has been generally acknowledged as an important part of late twentieth century theatre, site-specific performance. The key difference in respectability is surely that the earlier movements, though often professionally organized and directed, were almost exclusively actually performed by amateurs, while site-specific theatre has been essentially the work of professional organizations.

Site-specific theatre, like much experimental theatre of the twentieth century, had its origins not in the theatre world but in the world of art. In a reaction to the exclusivity and commodification of "museum" art, a number of artists in the late 1960s and early 1970s began to create works of art for specific public locations, outside the world of museum culture. By the later 1970s such work was widely recognized as a new approach and generally designated as "site-specific." Shortly after site-specific work began to appear in the art world, it also appeared in dance, inspired in part (like the contemporary happenings) by an interest in everyday activity as dance, and in part, like site-specific art, by a desire to move the art outside traditional and commercialized institutional structures. The Judson Poets Theater in New York was a center of such work, offering performances like Trisha

Brown's *Roof Piece* (1973), created to be performed simultaneously on a specific set of roofs in lower Manhattan.[34]

Although the term *site-specific* was not yet used, performances taking place in real-life nontheatrical locations characterized the work of a number of the leading British experimental companies created in the 1960s and 1970s, among them the People Show (founded in 1966), Pip Simmons (1968), Welfare State (1968), and IOU (founded in 1976). IOU, performing in abandoned houses, cathedrals, woods, mills, and on beaches and rooftops has said that in their work "the physical characteristics of the space condition the narrative, structurally and in content."[35] A center for such work in the 1970s was the Cardiff Laboratory Theatre in Wales, under the direction of Richard Gough. He created a series of what he called "special events," which he defined as "events for special times and places . . . disused churches, deserted beaches, abandoned country houses."[36] Two members of the Cardiff Laboratory Theatre, Lis Hughes Jones and Mike Pearson, left in 1981 to create the company Brith Gof, often cited as the first "site-specific" company in Great Britain and one of the first in Europe.

Certainly the application of this term, already well established in art and dance, to theatre, brought with it the idea of a work of art created for and theoretically fully understandable only within that location, but even more important than this formal concern was a political and social one. The very act of moving outside the conventional theatre, the concert hall, or the gallery was generally seen as representing a break not only with the practices of the past, but with their exclusivity and isolation from a more general public. Site-specific theatre in its early years in particular sought out physical locations that had specific relevance to working-class audience. "Engagement with site," reported Mike Pearson, "had here a political and proselytizing aspect."[37] Of course, this orientation was closely in harmony with the increasing politicization of the experimental theatre of Europe and the United States in the late 1960s and early 1970s, but it was also surely reinforced by a major shift taking place at this time in the study of history itself.

It was precisely at this time that the traditional "great man" view of history began to be seriously changed by "history from below" (the title of a key essay published in 1966 in the *Times Literary Supplement* by E. P. Thompson), which called for a shift in historical attention from the deeds of leading figures to the lives and social conditions of ordinary people. Precisely in this spirit, much early site-specific theatre turned away from figures like Abraham Lincoln or William Tell and from re-creations of famous battles, to build works based on everyday locations and everyday life. The reality evoked was the reality of that experience, not Elsinore but the working and living places of common folk. These locations were often disused or abandoned, allowing for their more easy adaptation to performance space, but also because the traces of their usage could still be seen and felt.

No one expressed this aesthetic better than Armand Gatti, one of the leading experimental dramatists in France at this period, and also one of the most politically engaged. In 1964 he decided to create a piece based on the life of Buenaventura Durruti, a freedom fighter in the Spanish Civil War and an excellent example of the growing interest in "history from below." As Gatti himself noted, Durruti was "a great man, although fortunately not in any biographical dictionary, and therefore not yet absorbed into mainstream thought." Note the "fortunately," which precisely situates Durruti as an example of the new historical orientation. To present Durruti's "historical truth," Gatti argued this character could not be presented in a theatre. "That would have been taking him out of his element, cutting him off from his context, from the air he breathed, from all that made him what he was."[38] Eventually Gatti determined that there were "only two places in the city that corresponded to his stature, to his language, to what he had been—factory or prison."

Gatti found a Belgian factory that was closing down and created his production in the recently abandoned spaces of this facility, in his words "theatricalizing the factory." His explanation is a striking example of Hugo's image applied not to settings of the great events of history, but to the life and work of the lower classes:

> [W]e had to make the discovery that with this kind of subject it's mostly the *place*, the architecture, that does the writing. The theatre was located not in some kind of Utopian place, but in a his-

toric place, a place with a history. There was grease, there were acid marks, because it was a chemical factory; you could still see traces of work; there were still work-clothes around; there were still lunch-pails in the corner, etc. In other words, all these left-over traces of work had their own language. These rooms that had known the labour of human beings day after day had their own language, and you either used that language or you didn't say anything. . . . That's why I wrote in an article, "a play authored by a factory."[39]

Clearly one can say, in the case of Gatti, that the factory was, in a sense, colonized by the theatre, but one could with equal justice say that the theatre has been colonized by the real space, the real objects, the real memories, and even the real language of the factory. It should also be noted that this production, like much site-specific theatre, utilized real elements that not only colonized the theatre but also the narrative material being represented. The historical Durruti in fact had no more connection with this specific factory than with the theatre, and thus the narrative became not exclusively his but that of the experience of modern factory labor. As Gatti notes, the place did the writing, not the dramatist nor the historians that wrote of the historical figure Durruti. The reality of the chemical factory itself overrode all of these.

As the term *site-specific* grew in popularity in the late twentieth century, so did its range of usage, until it came to mean almost any kind of theatrical performance taking place outside a conventional theatre building.[40] Some of these productions, such as the British artistic team of Ewan Forster and Christopher Heighes did not, like Gatti, place a narrative within a location, but like Gatti, sought to reveal the "language" of certain historically socially and architecturally significant buildings and locations, such as an art deco London settlement house in the 1997 piece *Preliminary Hearing* or the layering of architecture, landscape, and social history at Froebel College, Roehampton, in 1999's *The Curriculum*.[41] Still others, more like the original site-specific creators in the art world, sought to let locations inspire new original works.

For the most part, site-specific theatre has dealt with urban or at least with human-created sites, and thus, when historical material was involved, with human history. Often, as we have noted, this was human history involving those neglected by the grand historical narratives of the past and thus the reality involved was not only a physical but a social reality. With the rise of a new interest in environmental concerns, however, some site-specific work turned from constructed environments to natural ones. As we have seen, sunrises, night skies, bodies of water, forests, even breezes, have always been a part of exterior site-specific work, but it was not until after the environmental movement of the 1970s that artists began to produce major site-specific works which, although they might involve human actors, were primarily concerned with their audience's experience of the real natural world.

The most ambitious such artist was Canadian R. Murray Schafer, who from 1980 onward created a series of monumental works, primarily in natural locations, which together have made up his ongoing *Patria* project. Suzi Gablik, in her 1991 study of contemporary spiritually oriented experimental art, *The Reenchantment of Art*, cites Schafer as a leading example of those artists seeking spiritual renewal "by restoring awareness of our symbiotic relationship with nature." Schafer's goal, she suggests:

> is to cultivate a sense of merging with a vast ecology, with a scenery that can't be controlled, in order to understand that working with nature means working on nature's terms. By being responsive and listening to the natural world, Schafer hopes to make this understanding a practice through his art, which is paced by the rhythms of nature and linked with the greater movements of the cosmos.[42]

At the heart of Schafer's twelve-play cycle, begun in 1966 and not yet completed, are a number of units designed to be presented in Ontario's Haliburton Forest, where audiences gather in natural surroundings to see combinations of elements arranged by Schafer embedded in a landscape of forests and lakes. His intent, Schafer has explained, has been "to cultivate a sense of merging with a vast ecology, with a scenery that can't be controlled, in order to understand that working with nature means working on nature's terms. The art is paced by the rhythms of nature and linked with the greater movements of the cosmos."[43]

An important result of this is that the audience experiences not only real space but also real time, the time of nature. *Princess of the Stars*, the third play in the cycle, begins in darkness and features the forest and lake as dawn slowly comes, the major sounds provided by awakening birds. *The Spirit Garden* (*Patria* 10), first presented in 2005, involves planting seeds in its first section, and the harvesting of their products in the second, for which the audience must return six months later. Real products are really grown in real time and the spectators, if they chose, can also share in consuming them.

While *Patria* remains the most ambitious theatricalization of nature yet attempted, audiences have come during the past half century to accept the ability of theatre to claim almost any real location, as it can almost any activity, as part of its domain. Audiences have learned to accept the guidance of directors, scenographers, or actors in guiding them in the operations of this process. Even much more conventional productions are now susceptible to this process. Ever since 1961, the New York Public Theater has offered free productions of Shakespeare at its open-air Delacorte Theater in Central Park, a model for subsequent open-air Shakespeare all over the country. Although the Delacorte's stage is backed by an open picturesque romantic landscape, with trees, crags, a small pond, and a pseudo-Gothic castle, the Belvedere, all part of the part décor, for most productions this background is not evoked by the production, but simply adds to the general atmosphere, rather like the spacious vistas enjoyed by Greek audiences in many of the classical theatres such as that a Taormina, Sicily.

If an actor or director wishes to theatricalize these real surroundings, however, they can easily do so, and the audience will not only cooperate, but clearly enjoy the experience. A striking example of this occurred in a 2001 production at the Delacorte of Chekhov's *The Seagull*, starring Meryl Streep and Kevin Kline. The normally ignored Turtle Pond behind the theatre served as the backdrop for Konstantin's play in the first act, and later was thoughtfully contemplated by Kevin Kline, playing the writer Trigorin, for his line "There must be a lot of fish in that lake." The line aroused an appreciative chuckle from the audience, and even some scattered applause, something that surely would never occur in a regular theatre. A few native New Yorkers may have been amused by the knowledge that fishing is not allowed in the

Turtle Pond, as it is elsewhere in the park, but the majority of the audience surely were simply amused at the way that Kline, by applying the theatre's power of appellation, could convert what was clearly a real body of water into a part of Chekhov's imaginary world. Such is the power and the fascination of theatre's constant play of reality and illusion.

CHAPTER 4

Simon's Chair and Launce's Dog

For the most part, until a significant part of theatre production began to move, in modern times, outside traditional theatre structures, the scenery that surrounded the actor, even when closely modeled on real architecture and decoration, was in fact artificial, constructed for the occasion by the theatre itself. Only when theatrical production left its enclosed and artificial world did the scenic environment of the actor begin to present itself as both real and a part of the fiction. Of course, the actor has possessed this double quality from the beginning, bringing a real body into theatre's fictive universe.

An important part of theatrical production is located between these positions, the stage object or property.[1] Unlike the scenery, to which it is closely related, the property has, from the beginnings of theatre, often not been created in the theatre, but has been a product of the real world outside, brought into the theatre. Therefore, like the actor, it had an existence in the real world before appearing onstage, but being inanimate it has been far less likely than the actor to betray that other existence to the audience. An actor may be accidentally hurt, or simply forget a line onstage, thus disrupting the fictive world, while a property, once introduced, seems safely at home there. Exceptions do exist, however. Andrew Sofer speaks briefly but tellingly of "recalcitrant props," such as the gun that refuses to fire on cue, a break in the illusion, like the forgetful actor, that temporarily exposes the illusion and reveals the gun as a property.[2] There is also a special kind of "recalcitrant prop," which by its very nature provides a continual tension between the real world and the stage illusion. That is the onstage animal, to which I will return after considering the more conventional and ubiquitous properties that are inanimate.

On the whole, audiences are so accustomed to stage properties being imported from the outside world that unless their attention is called to that importation, it is absorbed into the general acceptance of the theatre's world of fiction. That dynamic gives particular power to one of the few cases I know of where this importation is specifically called to the audience's attention, in the play *Mnemonic* (2002), one of the major works of the leading contemporary British company, Complicite.

The work begins with a monologue by its author, Simon McBurney, identified in the text as the "Director" and gradually revealed in the production as a construct that is part McBurney, part a chorus, part a character in the play, and part a kind of modern Everyman. At the opening, however, when the play was originally presented, McBurney seemed to be appearing as himself, an actor and director well known in theatrical circles. He first appears casually dressed, walking onto a stage empty except for a chair and a small stone.

"Good evening, ladies and gentlemen," says McBurney. "Before we begin I'd like to say a few words about memory." The complex, several-minute monologue, which follows serves the same purpose as the traditional opening of the Sanskrit theatre, where the "director" greets the audience and leads them from their world into that of the play. For a time, however, we seem to remain in the real world we and McBurney share, and the onstage chair anchors this world. In McBurney's words:

> We experience memory through familiarity. How do we experience this? When we see something we know it sets off a chain of memory. For instance, perhaps I thought about my father because this was his chair. I *know* it. He sat on it. And so did my grandfather. In fact it's a chair I know very well because I've used it in another show. I have a proclivity for using personal props in my show. It was in a show called *The Chairs* by Ionesco.[3]

In this striking and perhaps unique speech, McBurney has called attention to the generally ignored fact that stage properties, like actors, not only have an extra-theatrical history, but in many cases a theatrical history as well. Of course, we know the first to be true of any actor and the second of any established actor like McBurney, but for the most part we overlook that many stage properties also have these same qualities. McBurney, we might almost say, has "outed" the chair in these other hidden lives.

Thus alerted to the real life of many stage properties, let us consider some of the ways in which this reality has calculatedly or not entered into the dynamics of theatrical production and reception. Although the Greeks were sparing in their use of properties, the few that appeared there had very strong narrative and symbolic use. Among the most famous is the urn carrying the ashes of Orestes wept over by Electra. One of the first recorded performance anecdotes concerns this stage property and the fusion of the real and the fictive in theatre. The renowned fourth-century Greek actor Polus is said to have achieved an unparalleled effect upon his audience when playing the title role in a revival of Sophocles's *Electra*, by removing from its tomb the urn of his own recently deceased son and using that to stimulate his own authentic emotion. Whether the story is factually true or not, it has been reported as true by most acting theorists and historians from the renaissance onward and is now an accepted part of Western theatre history.[4]

Generally the point of the story is that although the audience did not know that the urn in fact contained real ashes of the son of the real actor, they nevertheless responded to the reality of his emotion, which could not have been achieved without this foundation in the real.

It is almost universally assumed that the audience was not aware of Polus's stratagem, even though he had recently returned to the stage after a period of mourning over his son's death. Diderot, however, determined to demonstrate in his *Paradox* the superiority of technique over feeling, insists that Polus's presentation of emotion was in fact not that effective, but that the audience's reaction was due to their awareness of the real contents of the urn: "That prodigious effect, which I don't doubt took place, was not due either to Euripides' [*sic*] lines or to the actor's delivery, but to the sight of a grieving father who was bathing in his tears his own son's urn."[5] At any rate, the story places the conscious mixing of reality and fiction near the beginnings of theatre history, and if Diderot is correct, draws this audience into a conscious complicity in that mixing.

Polus's urn anticipates a much more famous memento mori—surely the most famous property in theatre history—Yorick's skull, around which swirl a dizzying mixture of truth and legend, reality and deception. Shakespeare was apparently the first dramatist to introduce a skull onto the stage, with such success that following *Hamlet*, skulls became one of the most popular stage properties of the Renaissance English stage. Sofer devotes a full chapter of his study of props to the Jacobean skull and to the dynamics which it set into motion, its unavoidable reality, and the sense of mortality it imposed upon the audience, reducing the characters around it, Hamlet included, to rhetorical shadows, theatrical props hollowed out by the overwhelming reality of this object. Speaking of the skull's appearance in *The Revenger's Tragedy*, one of the most extreme *Hamlet* offshoots, Sofer comments: "As in *Hamlet*, the reality of the skull flattens the very rhetoric Vindice uses to describe it."[6]

The vogue of skull plays faded with the Jacobean theatre, but the continuing popularity of *Hamlet* guaranteed the ongoing theatrical importance of the play's most famous property. Although its familiarity has removed from audience's much of the shock of its original appearance (covered with earth and worms, Sofer speculates), there is still a bit of a frisson in that the audience is rarely entirely sure if the object Hamlet is handling is a stage creation of plastic or papier-mâché, or in fact an the actual physical remains of a once-living being like themselves. Perhaps not surprisingly, theatre tradition has continually kept this important question ambiguous.

During the mid-nineteenth century, theatrical producers and audiences grew increasing interested in seeing real objects on stage. In 1878, a series of article on the history of stage props appeared in the London journal *Belgravia*, the third of which noted that in recent years theatre producers:

Moved by much fondness for reality, have shown a disposition to limit the labours of the property-maker, to dispense with his simulacra as much as possible, and to employ instead the actualities he but seeks to mimic and shadow forth. Costly furniture is now often hired or purchased from fashionable upholsterers. Genuine china appears where once pasteboard fabrication did duty—real oak-carvings banish the old substitutes of painted canvas stretched on deal laths and "profiled," to resort to the technical term, with a small sharp saw. The property-maker, with his boards and battens, his wicker-work and gold leaf, his paints and glue and size, his shams of all kinds, is almost vanished from the scene. The stage accessories become so substantial that the actors begin to wear a shadowy look . . . Real horses, real dogs, real water, real pumps and washing tubs are now supplemented by real bric-à-brac, bijouterie, and drawing room knick-knackery.[7]

It was during this period, when the theatre was growing increasingly interested in the presentation of real material of all kinds on the stage, that stories began to be circulated of real skulls appearing in productions of *Hamlet*. The American actor George Vandenhoff tells the story of a whimsical gravedigger actor who brought into the production the actual skull of a local preacher associated with the converted chapel where the company was playing, and so informed the actor playing Hamlet during the graveside banter.[8] Much better documented is the curious history of the skull of the American Shakespearian actor George Frederick Cooke. John W. Francis, the doctor called to attend Cooke on his deathbed, was both a theatre aficionado and a researcher of skulls, owning one of the largest collections in the city. He appropriated the actor's skull for his collection, and a headless body was buried. Some ten years later, a New York theatre company preparing a production of *Hamlet* asked to borrow a skull from Francis's well-known collection, and he seized the opportunity to return Cooke's skull to the stage. It subsequently appeared in a number of other productions of the play, reportedly including one starring the major American tragedian Edwin Booth. Nor was its provenance kept silent. Indeed, on occasion it received billing in the theatre program. Its stage career ended, it now reposes in Thomas Jefferson University's Scott Library in Philadelphia, having enjoyed what the university itself characterizes as "the longest active stage career in history."[9]

There are many versions of a story that Edwin Booth's father, Junius Brutus, possessed a skull that had been willed to him by a famous horse thief named Fontaine, although both whether Booth or his son Edwin either possessed or more importantly performed with such a skull is disputed. Rather better documented is the bequest to the Walnut Street Theatre in Philadelphia of the skull of John Reed, a lifetime gas-lighter there who, in his will, requested that his skull be bequeathed to the theatre to "represent the skull of Yorick."[10] It must be noted, however, that the Horace Howard Furness Memorial Library, where this skull now resides, claims that it was in fact originally donated to the Walnut Street Theatre by a Philadelphia pharmacist in the early nineteenth century. In any case, it remained in that theatre and was signed by all the major actors who performed there, among them Macready, Booth, Forrest, Cushman, Davenport, Murdock, and Brooks.[11] Most audience members of the period were doubtless unaware that this skull had a kind of celebrity status, although surely its performance lineage, recorded on its surface, gave it a special aura to the various actors who utilized it over the decades. At the end of the century Henry Irving notes that when audience members come backstage, "Yorick's skull is a property that the curious visitor naturally asks for." Not surprisingly, Irving is proud to exhibit "the genuine article, and no *papier-maché* counterfeit. It is ready to hand, for it rather recently made its reappearance in the study of Doctor Faustus. It is, in fact, a well-worn skull, that shines, from much handling, with a grisly sheen."[12] However, Irving does not mention its provenance.

The sense of the real carried by an actual skull was acknowledged by some of the leading actors and directors of the late twentieth century. When rehearsing *Hamlet* at the National Theatre in 1975, Peter Hall discovered the power of a real skull in rehearsal: "We rehearsed the graveyard scene this morning with a real skull. The actuality of the scene was immediately apparent: actors, stage management, everybody aware of a dead man's skull among us." Indeed, the effect was so powerful that it was decided not to bring the actual skull into the performance.[13] A similar situation developed at the Royal Shakespeare Company a little over a decade later. When the Polish pianist and composer Andre Tchaikovsky died in 1982, he bequeathed his skull to that company for use in *Hamlet*. In 1989, when Mark Rylance was rehearsing the role, he used the Tchaikovsky skull, with effects similar to those Hall reported. Again, however, plans to use it in performance were given up. Rylance's wife, Claire van Kampen explains:

> As a company we all felt most privileged to be able to work the Gravedigger scene with a real skull . . . However collectively as a group we agreed that as the real power of theatre lies in the complicity of illusion between actor and audience, it would be inappropriate to use a real skull during the performances . . ."[14]

Real water, real bodies, real chairs and tables, even real animals could apparently stand the strain of not significantly disrupting the illusory world of theatre, but the real skull of a known real person, it was felt, would too far test the limits of that world.

Apparently more successful was the dying wish of the Chicago improv-comedy star Del Close, who provided in his will for his skull to go to the Goodman Theatre for use in *Hamlet*, a desire he repeated on his deathbed to his executor, Charna Halpern. Several months after Close's death in 1999 the skull was presented to the Goodman in an elaborate ceremony, and it became a kind of Chicago legend, appearing, not in *Hamlet*, but in *Pericles*, *Arcadia*, and *I Am My Own Wife*, with appropriate acknowledgements in the programs. The Chicago theatre public, already familiar with Close in real life, seems to have found nothing troubling about his skull's subsequent appearances, either morally or theatrically, and, on the contrary, accepted it as a rather endearing and quirky piece of local lore.

Sadly, in July 2006, the *Chicago Tribune* challenged the authenticity of the skull, and after initial disclaimers, Halpern admitted that, unable to get permission from any Chicago lab to retain the skull, she had been forced to allow the entire body to be cremated. She then obtained a stand-in skull from an anatomical stock house, which she adjusted to more closely resemble Close, and gave to the Goodman. It is now on the artistic director's office bookshelf, awaiting future bookings, but not as Del Close.[15]

What then of the impression made upon Goodman audiences who believed they recognized the "real" skull of Close on a shelf in the production of *I Am My Own Wife*? This raises a question that one encounters in much of the presumed utilization of the "real" in theatrical productions, a question which arises particularly often in the case of "real" objects. In the late nineteenth century, when "reality" on stage became of central interest, objects such as Close's skull were often displayed (and advertised) as "real," which were, knowingly or unknowingly, not authentic. From a phenomenological point of view, however, that distinction does not affect reception. Benjamin's concept of the "aura" may be helpful here, which has been defined as "an elusive phenomenal substance, ether, or halo that surrounds a person or object of perception, encapsulating their individuality and authenticity."[16] Although Benjamin developed the concept of aura as the quality possessed by the authentic individual work of art, examples abound showing that aura is at least as much a product of perception as of creation. In my final chapter I will explore some of the implications of moving the distinction between the real and the fictional from the control of the producing organization to the assumptions and choices of the spectator.

As Simon McBurney's opening monologue in *Mnemonic* reminds us, the inanimate objects on the stage, like the actors who use them, simultaneously are related to several kinds of perceptive "reality," and the overlapping or clash of these different "realities" provides the tensions that are being explored in this book. Most centrally, a stage chair "represents" a fictional chair in the play being performed, just as an actor "represents" a character in that play. Secondly, just as a professional actor will appear as different characters in different plays, the stage chair can appear as different fictional chairs in different plays. Although this practice is less common in the contemporary commercial theatre, where the prevailing aesthetic requires that every new production, even of the same play, be created with new costumes and new furniture,[17] for most of theatre history, and in the noncommercial theatre today, costumes and props are kept in storage and can normally appear in a number of different productions. Thus McBurney can note that his audience members may be observed this chair before, in other productions, just as Chicago audiences were offered the "Close" skull in a variety of "roles."

Thirdly, the chair, like the actor, unless it is created in the theatre scene shop, which is not likely the case, has a history of a "private life" outside the theatre. The public has long been interested in the so-called private lives of actors, but until McBurney recounted the private life of his chair, few in the audience probably considered this level of the chair's reality. Scenic designers, on the other hand, are much more aware of this dimension. Tarek Abou el Fotouh, the designer for the noted Egyptian experimental company El-Warsha, observed that "Ordinary chairs have within them a sort of history, a link with the people and the place, and as such, are far richer than the poor, stunted fossilized clichés trapped within theatrical walls.[18] Occasionally a property can, like an actor, attain celebrity status in its private life, and I will consider such cases separately, but on the whole, that background is ignored in the theatre. For his first production, André Antoine pressed into service the furniture in his mother's living room, but this fact, although known to theatre historians, was surely not known to his original audience, nor would it, if known, had any appreciable effect upon their reception of the play.

This "private life" of properties remained essentially unconsidered until the late nineteenth century and the rise of interest in reality onstage, when enterprising producers often sought to provide an authentic "aura" for properties by tying them to a previous existence in the world outside the theatre. Until that time, the major way audiences could gain a sense of a property existing outside of the fictive world of the production was by its appearance in other productions. The average European theatre from the Renaissance onward tended to work with a very basic set of scenery and properties, which were used and reused in a variety of productions, allowing audiences to begin recognizing them a possessing an existence within the theatre similar to that of the recurring bodies of familiar actors. The English actor and manager Tate Wilkinson mentions in his memoirs, first published in 1790, a particular stage setting at the Covent Garden Theatre with Spanish figures and a folding door that he had first noticed there in 1737, and which still appeared in productions there from time to time at the time he was writing these memoirs, half a century later. "I never see those wings slide on," he remarks tellingly, "but I feel as if seeing my very old acquaintance unexpectedly."[19] Clearly the experience of seeing once again this inanimate "old acquaintance" worked in much the same way as seeing a familiar actor appear in a variety of roles.

Since actors in most theatres before the modern era were expected generally to provide their own costumes and their resources were limited, not only did costumes participate in such visual recycling, but could be associated with the particular actors who provided them. When, on the rare occasions where a particularly expensive costume, such as a royal robe, had to be created by the theatre itself, pure economics dictated that this same robe be pressed into service whenever possible. Thus, for the premiere of Schiller's *Die Jungfrau von Orleans* in 1803 at Weimar, both Goethe and Schiller had to appeal to the Duke for special funds for the creation of a "real coronation gown." Subsequently, the actor Eduard Genast reports, the gown "had to be passed down from king to king like a grandmother's wedding gown in the old days."[20]

This sort of undifferentiated recycling of stock material from a theatre's warehouse was stoutly opposed by the romantic theorists of the early twentieth century and by the realists who followed them, both of which envisioned a stage in which every element would be selected to contribute to the total artistic vision of each production and not utilized again. Nevertheless, custom and economy made this a vision unrealizable for most theatres. Even at the end of the nineteenth century, Nemirovich-Danchenko, Stanislavsky's codirector at the Moscow Art Theatre, reports that the sort of properties Wilkinson might have called "old acquaintances" had by no means disappeared. Moreover, audiences had become so familiar with certain of these that they, like certain actors associated with particular types of roles, brought with them certain expectations with each new appearance. Thus, Nemirovich-Danchenko reports, a certain tall lamp with a yellow shade became associated with "cozy love passages," while a curule chair in a "Gothic/Renaissance style," was in fact referred to by at least one director as the "culture chair."[21]

In more modern times, small theatres with limited budgets still recycle properties and costumes in the eighteenth-century manner, but there have also been important instances of major professional companies utilizing this practice, not out of economic necessity, but to encourage the audience to become aware of a particular object taking on a theatrical life of its own by reappearing in a series of productions. During the mid-1970s revival by Terry Hands of the entire cycle of the Shakespearian history plays by the Royal Shakespeare Company, each successive play used the same crown (which sometimes, like McBurney's chair, was left alone on stage at the beginning or end of one of the productions) but also, and more strikingly, an dazzling and quite historically inaccurate gold lamé coronation gown that, as the series continued, built up in the audience's mind a composite picture of the various kings who had worn it and of their almost uniformly unhappy fate. The robe thus took on a history and a signification of its own, outside the fictional universe of each particular play in which it appeared.

A number of leading experimental companies of the late twentieth century incorporated into their aesthetic a calculated recycling of production elements, again not for economic reasons, but in order to build up a web of associations linking together their productions but separated from the imaginary world or the particular theme or concern of any individual production. The leading Polish experimental artist and theatre-maker Tadeusz Kantor, like Simon McBurney, loved to bring into his productions items from his own life and experience and then reuse them in further productions, so that, like McBurney's chair, they took on a kind of independent existence. It was their simplicity, however, that appealed to Kantor, not their potential for developing meanings. Kantor's English editor and translator, Michal Kobialka, has characterized his theatre as one of "found reality." An important part of this reality was ordinary found objects, from schoolrooms, from secondhand shops, from Kantor's own home. Like the creators of the happenings, in which he was much interested, Kantor sought to do away with "illusion and imitation," seeking to "depict reality via reality." Thus he preferred objects without a history, "wretched objects," which, unencumbered as much as possible with other associations, represented "reality of the lowest rank," which he called the fundamental concept of all his work.[22]

Another major modern experimental company, the Wooster Group, shares both Kantor's fascination with found objects and his practice of reusing them in various productions. I have already noted the Wooster Group's interest in found material in creating their texts, but that interest extends to all aspects of the production. When Wooster Group chronicler David Savran compares the work of their director Elizabeth LeCompte to that of a "maker of collages," he could, with equal accuracy, be speaking of Kantor's use of found material. LeCompte, says Savran, "takes up a found object, a fragment, that comes onto the scene without fixed meaning, and places it against other fragments," creating a fluid collection of material whose parts are never "cemented" to each other, and none of which "ever becomes a fixed center."[23] Thus, a number of highly distinctive rolling stools, a red plastic flyswatter, and other everyday objects have appeared in a number of Wooster Group productions, contributing their own distinctive reality, like Kantor's crosses and rifles, to new collage configurations.

This dynamic of reusing particular objects in different plays, and thus potentially creating for them an alternative reality outside the fictional world of any particular performance doubtless goes back to the first companies that established ongoing productions and therefore began building up a stock of costumes and props, regularly reused, to support these. Thus the potential for an audience to recognize certain objects as moving about from play to play and thus suggesting a kind of extra-mimetic existence does not seem to have been remarked upon until the eighteenth century, and then only rarely. Another reality for these objects, outside the theatre entirely, does not really seem to have been considered until the romantic theorists began to consider how to bring the theatre closer to the experienced world.

For conservative artists and critics, especially in France, the center of neoclassicism, these forays into the real world were often seen as attacking the elevation and purity of art, which presumably set itself apart from the squalor and the randomness of everyday existence. It was his willingness to include such material that made neoclassical theorists like Voltaire condemn Shakespeare as an untutored barbarian, and by the same token made Shakespeare a hero and model to young romantics, who saw him as a champion of nature, truth, and reality.

This conflict was played out on the French stage in the years between 1790 and 1830 and the struggle was on several key occasions focused upon stage properties. I have already mentioned Talma's difficulties in presenting a real bed on the tragic stage in the productions of *Othello* and *Sylla*. Chairs had been utilized on the French stage, both comic and serious, since the first professional stages at the end of the seventeenth century. In tragedies, kings were allowed their thrones and the famous 1630 engraving of the farce players at the Hotel de Bourgogne shows a solitary chair as the single piece of furniture. Beds, however, were much more intimate and informal, especially in tragedies, and Talma overcame that concern only with great difficulty.

Ducis was the first French dramatist to adapt Shakespeare successfully for the French stage, but he did so only by removing almost all of the "barbarisms" objected to by Voltaire and others. Leaving the bed in *Othello* proved a mistake that he was forced to rectify, but he was well aware that any mention—or worse, display—of so realistic a property as a handkerchief was quite unacceptable in 1792. Accordingly, the token lost by his Helmonde is a diamond-studded headband, a property much more suited to a tragic heroine.

In romanticism's struggle to bring more reality to the French neoclassical stage, Desdemona's handkerchief became a key object. In 1829, more than thirty years after the Ducis *Othello* and the year before the famous battle over Hugo's romantic *Hernani* at the Comédie, a preliminary skirmish anticipating that battle was carried out by Hugo's fellow romantic, Alfred de Vigny, who presented at the Comédie an Othello far closer than Ducis to Shakespeare's original. Most notoriously, the diamond headband was replaced by the original handkerchief, the mere mention of which occasioned a riot. "One cannot imagine," reports Théophile Gautier, "the storm that burst out in the pit of the Théâtre Français when the Moor of Venice, grinding his teeth, demanded again and again that *handkerchief*, prudently called a *headband* in the Shakespearian imitation of the 'good Ducis.'" The scandal could not have been greater, said de Vigny, "if the Moor had profaned a church." The production was performed only once, and then closed by the authorities as a danger to public tranquility.[24]

With the coming of romanticism and its interest in local color and historicity, this attitude significantly changed. Hugo's concern about accurate settings was echoed in properties as well, and the history of such objects during the nineteenth century parallels that of the growing interest in historically accurate settings and costumes. The mid-century Shakespearian productions of Charles Kean in London showed this most clearly, selecting a specific historical period for each play and presenting only physical objects onstage that could be specifically documented for that period. Often documentation of these choices was included in the programs or printed texts of the plays. Thus the text of the 1856 *Winter's Tale* contained eleven sheets of drawings for specific stage properties. Leontes had to drink from a cup that was "of the proper pattern," while his child Mamillius was provided with a toy cart that had "its terra-cotta prototype in the British museum."[25] Archeological discoveries in the Middle East brought the same attention to historical spectacles set in that area. The artist and theorist E. W. Godwin, observed in 1864 that audiences now attend the theatre "to witness such a performance as will place us as nearly as possible as spectators of the original scene or of the thing represented, and this result is only possible where accuracy in every particular is assured."[26]

This attention to providing accurate objects for Leontes or Macbeth soon appeared as well in contemporary dramas of social life. In the decade after the Kean's revolutionary historical Shakespeare productions, Squire Bancroft and his wife applied the same attention to authentic objects at their Prince of Wales Theatre, with sofas, chairs, tables, and knickknacks identical to those in the living rooms of their public. In recognition of such details, their plays were popularly known as the "cup and saucer school" of drama. Kean's contemporary in Paris, the director Montigny at the Gymnase, astonished his audiences and forced new movement patterns on his actors by the simple expedient of adding placing a regular domestic table in the center of the stage, perfectly standard in a contemporary salon, but never in a stage setting.

Such displays of historical and contemporary "real" objects became standard on the late-nineteenth-century stage, reaching their apotheosis in the detailed realism of such prominent theatre figures as Irving and Belasco, as well as in avant-garde champions of naturalism like André Antoine, who shocked and astonished his audiences with such offerings as real running water from onstage faucets or real sides of meat hanging in an onstage butcher shop.[27] In almost every case, objects in this tradition, although presented as "real" did not, like McBurney's chair or Close's skull, claim an existence in the real world outside the theatre, although there are occasional exceptions. Throughout the century, melodrama theatres would, from time to time, titillate audiences by including real or claimed actual artifacts from notorious crimes. An early example was a production at London's Surrey Theatre in 1835, *The Gamblers*, based on a recent poisoning, posters for which promised that the audience would see on stage the actual sofa, chairs, and table of the murderer, the fatal jug that contained the poison, and, for good measure, the murder's actual horse and carriage.[28] For his staging of the attack on the Deadwood Stage, a feature of his Wild West Show for much of its history, Buffalo Bill used an actual coach in which he had himself ridden and which had in fact been attacked by Indians.[29] In 1888, a Boston fisherman, William Andrews, set off in his small boat, the *Dark Secret*, to cross the Atlantic. Although he was picked up drifting at sea some time later, his story gained sufficient publicity that it served as the basis for a production at Chicago's McVickers Theater in 1889, which advertised that "Captain William Andrews will appear in his twelve-foot dory in which he made his historic sea voyage."[30]

Even when tables, chairs, jugs, stagecoaches, and dorys are imported from the real world and advertised to audiences as such, they are not really "recalcitrant" (in Sofer's term) in their resistance to theatrical assimilation. Far greater resistance is clearly offered by the stage animal, an object brought onto the stage like a prop, possessing life and consciousness like an actor, but bearing a different relation to reality than either, and one that can never be completely controlled or predicted by the apparatus of theatre.

Certainly animal participants of all kinds were utilized in the circus-like spectacles of the Roman Empire, and animal acts of various kinds are well documented from the medieval period onward,[31] but as the theatre of the Renaissance developed, with an emphasis upon language, the disruptive power of nonhuman performers kept them for the most part to more casual street entertainments. Even Shakespeare, so opposed to the continental neoclassical tradition in many ways, expressed in *Henry V* a sentiment in perfect harmony with that more formal tradition: "Think when we talk of horses, that you see them / Printing their proud hoofs i' the receiving earth."[32] The purely verbal evocation of animals apparently did not extend to dogs, however,

Shakespeare creating in *Two Gentlemen of Verona* one of the most famous of all stage dogs, Launce's dog Crab. Moreover, the recalcitrance of Crab as a stage object seems built into the text. As Bert States observes:

> Anything the dog does—ignoring Launce, yawning, wagging its tail, forgetting its 'lines'—becomes hilarious or cute because it is doglike.[33]

Crab was not the first dog recorded on the Elizabethan stage, although his predecessors clearly served in a less contributory role. A pack of foxhounds invaded the stage in a Cambridge performance of Euripides' *Hippolytus* as early as 1552, and several subsequent plays offered characters with pet greyhounds, among them Guarini's popular romantic tragicomedy *Il Pastor Fido*.[34] Horses, a considerably more ambitious innovation, do not seem to have appeared on the English stage until 1668, when Pepys records horses being "brought upon the stage" of the King's Playhouse for a revival of Shirley's *Hyde Park*.[35] Much more surprisingly, a 1682 revival of Corneille's spectacle-drama *Andromède* created a sensation in solidly neo-classic Paris by featuring a live horse as Pegasus, suspended above the stage by wires.[36]

It was not until a century later, however, that horses became an important part of the theatrical scene in London and Paris. Central to this development was the circus pioneer Phillip Astley, active in both cities, who began as a trick rider but in 1771 created a comic narrative about an inept horseman, *The Taylor Riding to Brentford*, which became a standard clown act in circuses and minor theatres for much of the next century. Out of Astley's work grew a whole genre of equestrian drama in England and France, primarily offered at specially designed hippodrome theatres combining traditional stages with circular areas for equestrian display. Sometimes the horses were portrayed "naturalistically," pulling chariots or providing cavalry for mock battles, but the most famous performing horses were trained to perform a variety of surprising, often apparently heroic acts, even becoming the central figures in their spectacle-melodramas. In *Le Cheval du Diable*, for example, presented in 1946 at the Paris Cirque-Olympique, the horse Zisco was hailed by Théophile

Gautier as an "actor of the first rank." The horse "carries of a princes at a spanking rate . . . unmasks a villainous knight, drags him with his teeth before the Court and kicks him to death, routs a pack of walruses and Polar bears . . . searches for the Emperor's child in a brigand's lair which can only be reached by crossing a bridge of iron chains overhanging a precipice; dances the tarbuka before the wonderstruck populace of Damascus, and hurls himself into Hell at an infernal gallop."[37]

It was activities such as these that particularly delighted nineteenth-century audiences, and a wide variety of animals participated in them. Although dozens of London and Paris theatres offered such fare, Paris' Cirque-Olympique was the center of such activity. There, in the early years of the century, the stags Coco and Azor leapt across chasms, ascended narrow ramps, and plunged from high platforms. There, in the 1830s and 1840s, the elephants Baba and Kiouny played musical instruments, caught apples, balanced stools, and in a famous scene in the 1845 *Les Eléphants de la Pagode*, sat down to tea, ringing for a servant to bring it and then daintily partaking.[38] More dangerous animals enjoyed a great vogue in the 1830s. In *Le Lion du desert* (cirque, 1839), "A lion and a panther performed, on a stage filled with extras . . . tricks as demanding as those carried out by the best-trained poodles and monkeys, and this without anything separating them from the spectators, not even a metal wire, not even a cleverly concealed rope; they are in full liberty."[39]

This strong interest in unusual and unexpected actions performed not only by dogs and horses, but even by such less likely creatures as stags, elephants, or panthers, recalls the important distinction made concerning human acting by Jean Alter between referential and performant functions—the former being the mimetic, narrative-bearing creation of the stage character—the latter being the non-mimetic specific skills displayed by the actor. Although both are usually in the service of the dramatic action, the second, exhibiting skill and technique, by that same token always potentially suggests the "real" actor who must actually have these skills. Thus, in addition to bringing a certain reality to the theatrical event simply by being a living body drawn from the nontheatrical world, the actor, when he or she calls attention to his or her physicality by the display of unusual technical skills, displays his or her non-mimetic "reality" in another way. The same distinction may be made in the case of animal performers. A real horse ridden onstage in a late-nineteenth-century historical drama was essentially a property, like its rider's helmet and shield. Its mimetic function was essentially like that of a table or chair. When Azor executed special leaps and dives, however, the performant quality of his action was emphasized.

Even the unusual architecture of the hippodrome reinforced this double functionality. In 1752 the British Licensing Act, which restricted the number of repertoire of English theatres, was extended to include the London suburbs, forbidding the minor theatres in these areas to produce regular spoken drama. Except for the brief period from 1791 to 1806, similar restrictions were placed on the minor theatres of Paris. One of the results of these restrictions was that many small theatres circumvented them by adding features to their productions that presumably removed them from the domain of legitimate drama. The three most common circumventions were the addition of music, of acrobatics, and of animals. Dominating the latter area were equestrian displays. These formed the basis of the first modern circus, created in London in 1768 by Philip Astley, who soon varied these entertainments by adding clowns and acrobats. In 1782, his monopoly in such entertainments was challenged by Charles Dibden's Royal Circus, the first building to bear that title. The Licensing Act theoretically restricted the fare in these two theatres to animal and acrobatic acts, but both took advantage of the dramatic potential of both to present popular mixtures of theatre and physical display.

The Royal Circus introduced a striking architectural innovation, adding a full theatrical stage to one side of its traditional circus ring. On this, Dibden planned to present "spectacles, each to terminate with a joust or a tilting-match, or some other grand object," to be performed in the ring.[40] Although it took several years for this theatre to create such integrated spectacles, Astley immediately recognized the potential of this arrangement and as early as 1784 added a conventional stage to one side of his arena as well. Although Astley also opened a circus building in Paris in 1783, it was only a simple circle, and Paris did not see a combination ring and stage theatre until Astley's rival, Antonio Franconi,

opened his Cirque-Olympique, the most famous of the hippodrome theatres, in 1807. During the next half-century, the great
age of the hippodromes, the leading such theatres were all built as
combination rings and stages, a striking physical confirmation of
their ongoing double focus upon mimetic illusion and the display
of real physical achievement.

Although horses were the specialty of the hippodrome theatres like the Cirque-Olympique, the favored performing animal
on more conventional nineteenth-century stages, from small
melodrama houses to major venues like Drury Lane and Covent
Garden, was the performing dog, and, not surprisingly, in these
more narrative-driven houses, it was the performant aspect of
these dogs that was most often emphasized. Like the famous
horse Zisco, they braved dangers of fire, water, and heights to save
their masters, expose villains, and rescue helpless children. The
first great canine star was Carlo, who first appeared in a spectacle
melodrama, *The Caravan*, at Drury Lane in 1803. Carlo's leap
into a river to save a drowning child and other such feats were
much admired and he was greeted upon his entrance like leading
actors, with great applause and shouts of his name (to which he
often responded with excited howls). The occasional onstage
emergence of the "real" dog was delightedly reported by the
newspapers—his occasional refusal to share his food with a sup-
posedly hungry prisoner, his preventing a soldier from throwing
the child into the river, his occasional lying down onstage and
refusing to move. In fact, however, such incursions of the real
only added to his appeal. No two performances were identical and
some people reportedly came to see the play again and again to
see what unexpected behavior Carlo might next display.[41] Carlo
was a great success at Drury Lane, star of a number of dramas
between 1803 and 1811, and even the subject of a fictional autobiography for children, *The Life of the Famous Dog Carlo*, published in 1804.

The passion for dog dramas did not subside until the 1880s, by
which time Carlo had been followed by several generations of
similar performers. The most famous of these plays, an enormous
international success, was *The Dog of Montargis* by René Charles
Guilbert de Pixérécourt, the father of the modern melodrama,
first presented in Paris in 1814, where it enjoyed an uninterrupted

run until 1834. It was translated into English the year of its opening, into German in 1815, and played throughout Europe and in the United States for decades, and in England until the 1880s. Most famously, it occasioned in 1817 the departure of Goethe from the direction of the theatre in Weimar, which he and Schiller had made into one of the most respected in Europe. The Weimar theatre productions had a strong neoclassical orientation, and if the French national theatre found the display of so "real" an object as a handkerchief on stage a challenge to the elevated realm of art, a live dog was even more outrageous. Goethe informed his sponsoring Duke that he must choose between himself and the dog, like the handkerchief in Paris, triumphed.

Toward the end of the century, animal plays of this sort disappeared from the legitimate theatres, as did the taste for the sort of melodramatic spectacle they represented. Performing animals, even in dramatic actions, did not disappear, but moved into the world of circus, vaudeville, and variety entertainment. In part, this was a result of the growing interest in realism, which found the exploits of figures like Carlo or Zisco too "theatrical" for contemporary taste. Henceforth, it was the referential instead of the performant orientation which characterized the use of onstage animals. Thus we have the famous rabbits introduced by Beerbohm Tree in 1911 into the detailed naturalism of his *Midsummer Night's Dream*, with trails of bran amid the trees, insuring that they did not depart from their use as living properties.[42] Almost a century later, in 2008, another devotee of detailed stage realism, Peter Stein, presented for his production of Kleist's *The Broken Jug*, a scrupulous re-creation of the French genre engraving that had inspired the play, adding to the rustic interior a number of chickens chased about the stage by maids to open the production.

Such examples of animals used to provide local color, not uncommon a century ago, are rarely seen today, and performing animals like Carlo not at all. One of the most ambitious attempts to create a modern equivalent of the animal spectacles of the early twentieth century was the 1990 *Endangered Species* by Martha Clarke, an American experimental director who has regularly pushed the boundaries of both dance and theatre. Her piece opened the annual festival of experimental work at the prestigious Brooklyn Academy of Music, the interior of which was converted into a ring and stage space strongly suggesting a traditional hippodrome theatre. Here, Clarke mixed human actors with an elephant, horses, and other animals in a symbolic work about ecology and extinction, seeking "to put animals on stage without exploiting them" and to "use elements of the circus without making it into a circus."[43]

In fact, the sort of display of real animals onstage that delighted audiences at London's leading theatres a century before was dismissed by critics and publics in terms somewhat reminiscent of Goethe's condemnation of a dog on the Weimar stage. Associations with the circus and such popular forms were too strong and considered unsuitable in a theatre devoted to experimental high art. The show did not even complete its scheduled run, and Martha Clarke did not direct another production for the next five years.

In the contemporary theatre, both traditional productions and most experimental work are generally subject to quite strict artistic control, and the potential recalcitrance of an animal discourages their use. Dogs, the animal most easily managed, are seen most often, but are almost never given the kind of encouragement to improvise that Shakespeare gives Launce's Crab. Sebastien Nübling's brilliant 2012 *Orpheus Descending* provided a powerful recent example of the use of live dogs in a classic text. Jabe Torrence, the dying, despotic Klansman who rules the town, is accompanied by a silent but sinister Doberman, a drawing of whose head appears on the uniforms of Torrence's evil followers. In this Satanic Southern town, the black Doberman seems a true hellhound, and when he sits alone onstage at the end he clearly represents the triumph of the forces of darkness. The fact that he is a living animal, representing a breed associated with ferocity and aggression clearly is intended, successfully, to give the audience a feeling of uneasiness that no abstract symbol of evil power could as easily convey.

An almost opposite but equally powerful effect is achieved by the appearance of a live puppy near the end of Simon Stephens's 2012 prize-winning *The Curious Incident of the Dog in the Night-Time*. When it was revived, with great success, in New York in 2014, *New York Times* critic Ben Brantley, displaying the traditional critical uneasiness with live animals, misses entirely the symbolic importance of the puppy and its reflection of the emotional and physical relationships in the play. He comments: "I am sorry to tell you that a winsome puppy figures in its denouement."[44] There is nothing to feel sorry about, however. The puppy, like Nübling's Doberman, becomes a powerful symbol both of the complex emotional relationships in the play and the worldview of its unconventional young hero. He is a more than worthy successor of Carlo and Crab.

CHAPTER 5

All the World's a Stage

This study began with a brief survey of historical changes in the concept of mimesis in the theatre, with particular emphasis upon how this concept has connected the material presented onstage with the spectator's previous experience with objects and processes in the "real" world outside the theatre, the "natural" world. In its most straightforward form, most famously articulated by Hamlet, theatre "holds a mirror up to nature," so that what is seen on stage is presumably instantly recognized as a more or less faithful, if artificial copy of that natural world. Other arts involve mimesis to some extent, but the theatre is unique in the extent to which its component parts are or can be directly taken from nature and used it the process of representation. The physical body of the actor, always existing both as a living being in the real world and as a representation of a fictive being in the theatrical world, has always been at the center of this negotiation, although almost any part of the theatrical world can operate on the double level of fiction and reality.

In many theatrical traditions, especially the more formal or stylized ones, the "real" element in this balance is deemphasized, but in others, creators of theatre have called attention to it, and even made the tension between the real and fictive an important part of the theatrical experience. The rise of romanticism and its successor realism in the Western theatre created conditions particularly favorable to the exploration of this tension, and during the past century or so the development of experimental and avant-garde theatre has been even more extensively concerned with it.

Despite the enormous variation even within the Western theatre, with which I have been primarily concerned, the dynamics of mimesis and the utilization of the real in the theatre have taken place within an overarching concept of theatre itself that has remained essentially unchallenged until relatively recent times. According to this concept, a group of spectators gather to watch a performer or performers present an imaginary story by means of enactment. Eric Bentley, in his often-quoted "minimal definition" of theatre, removed even the narration of a story, retaining only mimesis itself: "A impersonates B while C looks on."[1] From classical times onward, this dynamic was reinforced by the architecture of buildings especially created for theatrical performances, which, despite many variations, always minimally retained a distinct spatial division between the area where A impersonated B (the stage) and that where C looked on (the auditorium). During most of the theatre's history there have been occasions where this sharp division was challenged, but the occasions were rare and almost invariably with a distinct aura of calculated or spontaneous aggression (calculated, in the case of plays like Beaumont and Fletcher's *Knight of the Burning Pestle* [1607] wherein "audience members" invade the stage and take over the action, or spontaneous, as in the English Old Price Riots of 1809 when real audience members really invaded the stage).

With the rise of romanticism, even more strikingly with realism, and more strikingly still with many of the experimental undertakings in the theatre from the beginning of the twentieth century onward, audiences were more and more often encouraged to recognize material onstage as actually originating in their world, not as simply imitating or reflecting it. The previous chapters have provided both examples of this dynamic and at least some of the varied motivations for it. The traditional audience is often spoken of as playing a passive role, but this is only true to a certain extent and in any case focuses on upon physical activity. The performance and indeed the process of mimesis itself demand the active participation of the spectator both intellectually and emotionally. It is only what Shakespeare calls the "imaginary puissance" of the spectator or Coleridge the "willing suspension of disbelief" that actually allows mimesis, and the theatrical illusion, to take place at all. Bentley thus vastly underplays the role of C, who must not merely passively "watch," but take upon him or herself the task of giving theatrical meaning to the material being presented. It is the recognition of this critical role of the spectator that lies at the basis of modern reception theory, which recognizes the theatre experience as a co-creation of the producing apparatus and its audience.

Even so, the audience has traditionally, from classical times onward, and is still, for the most, part physically situated within the theatre experience in such a way as to continue and reinforce the reductive vision of Bentley, as the passive observer of the activities of others, the passive consumer of their product. From the point of view of the present study, however, the most important function of the audience is to provide the grounding of the "real." For any stage element—the actor, the properties, the costumes, the scenery, to be seen as "real," it must be perceived as belonging in recognizable measure not to the fictive world of the theatre but to the world in which the audience exists outside the theatre, and although the theatrical apparatus can emphasize this quality, it is the audience who ultimately must decide if and to what extent any stage phenomenon is to be seen as "real." From the beginning of the twentieth century onward, however, as we have seen, a significant part of experimental theatre has challenged the traditional dividing line between the "real" world of the auditorium and the mimetic world of the stage, although it still remains the spectator who must make the final decision as to which of these worlds, or what blend of them, will determine the status of any theatrical element.

To state the situation in these terms, however, is to reinscribe the apparently unbreakable binary upon which theatre is based—that of the real world and the mimetic world, that of the spectators and that of the actors. During with twentieth century, however, when artistic experimentation continually sought new directions, this binary also became significantly challenged. Bert States argued that theatre must continue to make further "bites into reality" in order "to sustain itself in the dynamic order of its own ever-dying signs and images." In another key passage, States suggests that: "Theatre is the medium, par excellence, that consumes the real in its realist forms: man, his language, his rooms and cities, his weapons and tools, his other arts, animals, fire, and water—even, finally, theatre itself."[2] The dynamics of this consumption has been the subject of much of the present study, but as we draw toward the end, I want to emphasize that one of the most striking modern extensions of this process has been experiments in the theatrical consumption of the audience, and indeed of the audience's own extra-theatrical world and the "reality" of which it is composed.

Pirandello is generally thought of as the pioneer in involving the audience in the stage action, and of course this device was highly important to his innovative theatre. In fact, a number of dramatists from earlier periods anticipated him in this practice—for example, Beaumont and Fletcher in their 1607 *Knight of the Burning Pestle* or Ludwig Tieck in his experiments with what was called romantic irony, such as his 1797 *Puss in Boots*. Although this device continues to be utilized, there has surely never been a significant part of the "real" audience who were fooled, or fooled very long, into thinking that their presumed representatives in these plays were in fact actual audience members like themselves.

During the twentieth century, however, real audience members were, for the first time in significant numbers, brought, willingly or unwillingly, into the dramatic action. Important examples of both occur early in the century, a period of intense theatrical experimentation in Europe. One of the earliest, and most extreme attempts to introduce unwilling spectators into the theatrical action surely occurred during the futurist "evenings." Filippo Marinetti, the leader of the movement, famously suggested a number of strategies for achieving this affect in the key futurist manifesto, "The Variety Theatre" in 1913:

> Introduce surprise and the need to move among the spectators of the orchestra, the boxes, and the balcony. Some random suggestions: spread a strong glue on some of the seats, so that the male or female spectator will remain stuck to the seat and make everyone laugh (the damaged dinner jacket or toilette will be paid for at the door).—Sell the same ticket to ten people: resulting in traffic jams, bickering, and wrangling.—Give free tickets to men and women who are notoriously unbalanced, irritable, or eccentric and likely to provoke an uproar with obscene gestures, pinching women, or other freakishness. Sprinkle the seats with dusts that provoke itching, sneezing, etc.[3]

Shock being an important ongoing element of the twentieth-century avant-garde, unwilling audience members are still, a century after the futurists, being similarly thrust into the theatrical event,[4] but far more common during that century and today have been productions which incorporated willing spectators into the physical world of the dramatic action. Such activity was particularly widespread in the Russian Revolutionary theatre at the opening of the century, almost simultaneous with futurism but with motives for audience involvement as different as were the results and the experiences themselves.

I have already mentioned the most famous revolutionary spectacle, the 1920 *Storming of the Winter Palace*, the massive crowds of which mixed actors, actual participants in the original battle, and spectators in a shared experience and space. At a time when theatre creators were seeking new modes to express a new society, the mixing of spectators and actors often was used to suggest the proposed communal nature of that society. Thus actors would mingle with spectators in real locations like the square in front of the Winter Palace, while spectators would mingle with actors on theatre stages, sharing the theatrical settings and the simulated encampments of revolutionary battlefields.

The political motivation for this bringing of audiences into the theatrical world stage came in significant measure from a seemingly highly unlikely source, Rousseau's famous attack on the theatre in his 1758 *Lettre à d'Alembert*. Like Plato, Rousseau distrusts mimesis itself, which he considers hides the truth of nature and substitutes for it shadows, and often injurious ones. He does not condemn "public shows and entertainments," but, likely in conscious imitation of Plato, he rejects keeping people "shut up in a gloomy cavern, there to sit for hours motionless, silent and inactive," but calls instead for spectacles "in the open air, in the face of heaven," where "the spectators themselves may be made actors," enjoying their common humanity and freedom.[5]

These pronouncements first made a major cultural impact during the French Revolution, where the great revolutionary festivals, conceived of as mass participatory events with strongly theatrical overtones, were profoundly influenced by Rousseau's ideals. Although theatre artists participated in these festivals, masses of spectators attended, and symbolic elements were centrally employed, these celebrations more resembled major modern parades and political rallies than theatrical entertainments. A distinctly more theatrical aura surrounded the festivals of the Russian Revolution, which were directly inspired by those of the French Revolution. Again masses of the public were involved, but this time as active participants. A central concern of theatre theorists and practitioners of the Russian Revolution was the involvement of the entire society in the creation of the new order, with the old division of actors and spectators widely seen as a reflection of the old class society.

The Russian revolutionary interest in using theatrical participation as a means of instilling and encouraging support for social change remained an important element in experimental theatre from the early twentieth century onward. Among the most important employers of this strategy was Bertolt Brecht, whose *Lehr-stücke* (teaching plays) were based upon the principle of merging audiences and actors, so that the experience of actually participating in the play provided participants with new political insight. Brecht's strategy inspired another major politically engaged director and theorist of the twentieth century, Augusto Boal, who created a variety of dramatic techniques in which the traditionally passive spectator became the physically and intellectually engaged "spec-actor." His "Forum theatre," in which "the participant has to intervene decisively in the dramatic action and change it,"[6] during the late twentieth century inspired audiences to move into performance contexts in politically oriented experimental theatres around the world.

During the late 1960s and early 1970s a different sort of experimental theatre also sought in various ways to absorb and incorporate its spectators. Richard Schechner provided the first major theoretical discussion of this practice in his 1973 book *Environmental Theater*. A key chapter in this work is called "audience participation," a phenomenon that Schechner notes is rapidly growing in importance in the Western theatre, although, he asserts, it has remained "dormant since medieval times."[7] While this is not strictly correct, there is no question that the movement of the real bodies of the audience into the sort of mimetic space traditionally reserved for actors sharply increased in the Western theatre in the early twentieth century, received new attention in the 1960s and 1970s, and continues to grow in importance today. Schechner's explanation for this phenomenon is that in the increasingly closed and unresponsive system of modern media culture, audience participation is an attempt to open the system and make feedback possible.[8] This argument very much reflects the emancipatory spirit of its time with its enthusiasm for real, unmediatized experience, and although this position has been seriously undermined since, as in the discussions around the ability to escape from mediatization raised by Philip Auslander's 2002 book *Liveness*, the vision of such emancipation was certainly one of the stimuli for audience participation in the late twentieth century.

Clearly Schechner's analysis, and his own work involving audiences from this period, most notably *Dionysius in '69* (1969) grows from quite different concerns than the political theatre of Brecht or Boal, although as the century passed these various traditions became more and more interwoven. Significantly, Schechner, discussing his own experiments in participatory theatre, does not mention the politically oriented work of Brecht or the Russians in this direction, but instead traces a genealogy from experimental artists John Cage and Allen Kaprow, whose influence on participatory theatre, he asserts "cannot be overestimated." He quotes approvingly from Kaprow's 1966 axioms for happenings, among them that "(A) The line between art and life should be kept as fluid, and perhaps as indistinct as possible," and "(F) It follows that audiences should be eliminated entirely."[9]

Of course, critical to Kaprow's theory was that happenings should be always separate from theatre, which he felt could significantly compromise the line between "art and life." Schechner's environmental theatre, on the contrary, explored how this vision of the blurring of art and life and of the boundary between actor and spectator could be achieved within the theatre. His citation of Cage and Kaprow shows that his concern was not in the engaged, political theatre, but much more in the experimental tradition of twentieth-century performance that sought to explore and expand the boundaries of art, very frequently by introducing elements of the real or by more directly involving the spectator. Both strategies are already present early in the century in the work of the futurists and Dadaists, and, more recently, the work of Jerzy Grotowski, an enormous influence on Schechner and many of his generation, which explored in a wide variety of ways the elimination of the passive, "invisible" spectator. Although Grotowski did not directly involve spectators as did many of his international followers later in the century, he often incorporated their real bodies into his early theatrical works, so that they became, most famously, inmates in the mental hospital which was the setting of his 1962 *Kordian* or as guests around Faust's table in his 1963 *Doctor Faustus*.

Schechner's designation of this type of theatre as "environmental" opens up other important associations outside the world of theatre. During these same years, environmental art was being established as an important new direction in contemporary art. Like much of the experimental theatre of this period, environmental art was in large part a challenge to traditional modes of production, and to the traditional class-based exclusivity of museum culture. Phenomenologically, it also radically changed the physical experience of viewing a work of art. Instead of the relatively passive experience of viewing a painting or even a piece of sculpture in a museum, the viewer of an environmental art work must actively engage with it, enter its own space, clearly a process similar to that of environmental theatre.

During the mid-1970s, a closely related term began to appear first in the art world and subsequently in theatre, *site-specific*, applied at first to works created for a specific location, but later, in theatre, more and more generally applied to almost any performance taking place outside of a traditional theatre structure. And yet, although traditional theatre spaces were abandoned by such productions, traditional actor-audience relationships were usually maintained. Thus productions in stone quarries, abandoned factories, and open fields normally had separate areas for actors and spectators, the latter frequently seated on bleachers or platforms created for the occasion.

Bringing the audience directly onstage, one important element of twenty-first-century experimental theatre, was still rarely seen, but one important exception occurred at London's National Theatre in 1984. Then-director Peter Hall, over the objections of his leading actor Ian McKellen and others, decided to bring audience members onstage to portray the Roman citizens in his production of *Coriolanus*. Twenty years later, McKellen still recalled this experiment as an unhappy betrayal of a basic theatrical feature:

> Hall placed about 30 members of the audience on the stage. They were expected, under the direction of the cast, to respond to the action. This they either totally failed to do—blocking my first entrance, for example, too nervous to interfere by shifting their ground so the arrogant Caius Martius had to walk ignominiously round them—or they joined in too enthusiastically, waving or chatting amongst themselves at inappropriate moments. After 30 performances I was fed up with all this and, having established that Irene [Worth] and the rest of the cast agreed, I wrote a memo to Peter asking for his permission to try a couple of performances with the audience where they belonged, i.e. not on the stage with the actors.

Peter refused, accusing me of "rather undermining everything I think about the production."[10]

During the 1980s a more active, though not necessarily more involved, audience arrangement developed, often (especially in England) called a "promenade" production. Here, the production utilizes a number of different locations and the audience moves from one location to another to follow the action. Although the term is new, this general arrangement is certainly not. It was common in the medieval theatre, as Schechner noted in calling such theatre "environmental." Although, as Schechner noted, long "dormant" in the West, promenade-style productions are not unfamiliar in other theatre traditions. Many of the Indian Ramlilas, for example, dramatic presentations dealing with the life of Rama and dating back for centuries, utilize variations of promenade performance, most notably, the Ramlila of Varanasi, presented in its modern promenade form since 1830.

Although *Dionysius in '69* concluded with actors and audiences led by Dionysius out of the theatre into the streets, the promenade form did not really begin to appear in the Western theatre until the following decade. In 1975 the Living Theatre required audiences in Ann Arbor, Michigan, to walk to different symbolic sites for its 1975 *Six Public Acts*, viewing a ritual of the Golden Calf before a bank, a blood ritual at a military memorial, and so on.[11] Maria Irene Fornés's 1977 *Fefu and her Friends* was hailed as a major innovative work not only for its strong feminist message but for its unusual staging. In the second part of the play, the audience was divided into four groups, moving through four different locations in different order until everyone had seen all parts of the play, though in different order (a device copied by Ivo van Hove in his 2014 *Scenes from a Marriage*). A more elaborate development of this device was seen in John Krizanc's *Tamara*, created in Toronto in 1981, revived in Los Angeles in 1984, and in New York in 1987. For each production, ten rooms of the palatial villa of the Italian author Gabriele d'Annunzio, were created in some elegant, preexisting Victorian building—in New York, it was the Park Avenue Armory. There was not a single line of action, but multiple scenes playing simultaneously, so, although audience members could not move totally freely, they could freely decide which of a number of these scenes they would watch and in what order. Thus, unlike the audience of *Fefu*, no audience member could see all the material being offered in any single visit, but would assemble an individual experience by multiple choices of alternative scenes. This multi-location variation on site-specific theatre grew in popularity through the 1980s, even inspiring companies specifically devoted to such work such as the "environmental" Ensemble Theatre created in Vermont in 1984, whose most famous production was their 1986 staging of Thornton Wilder's *Our Town*. Each act was presented in a different building located around the village green of Wilderesque Middlebury, Vermont, and audience members moving from one location to another passed staged outdoor vignettes of village life illuminated by lantern light.[12]

On the whole, the audience experiences in promenade productions of the 1970s and 1980s were fairly tightly controlled in terms of when and where the audience went and what they saw. Thus the outdoor vignettes passed by the Vermont spectators, although located in nontheatrical space, were clearly recognized and experienced as part of the controlled fictive world of the production. Productions of this sort have remained popular into the new century, especially in England, the United States, and Australia, with companies—some of whose names (One Step at a Time Like This, founded in Melbourne in 2001; Walkabout, founded in Chicago in 1999)—indicate their particular interest in work of this type. Although some productions of companies like these still exercise the sort of artistic control over the experience of their spectators normally found in the past century, a far greater degree of autonomy has been accorded the audience in more recent ambulatory work. Audiences have been given increasingly greater freedom in constructing their own experience, selecting what parts of the offered material they will observe and in what order, and in the most open experiments, encouraged to directly interact with the world being presented, thus becoming true co-creators of the experience.

Walking, however, remains the dominant mode of promenade movement, and has been the bases of the so-called immersive theatre of the London-based company Punchdrunk. Punchdrunk has abandoned traditional theatre spaces to create elaborate indoor environments in multi-floored abandoned structures of all sorts, staged static and moving scenes at different places within them, and then given audiences the freedom to wander about and explore these environments as their inclinations lead them. They may follow and watch the actors, but they may also have drinks at a bar, read books in a library, or even sleep in one of the production's beds. One thing they are instructed not to do, however, at least in *Sleep No More*, the company's signature project, is interact with, or even speak to, either actors or other audience members (all of whom are required to wear distinctive masks). Thus the production seeks a highly personal, almost private, experience.

Created in London in 2003, *Sleep No More* moved to New York for a five-week run in the spring of 2011. Its phenomenal success, however, caused the run to be extended repeatedly, and it is still, as of this writing, in the spring of 2015, playing to sold-out houses, and the inspiration for countless other "immersive" productions. The apparent freedom to construct their own experience offered by Punchdrunk and others gave particular prominence to a 2007 essay by Jacques Rancière, entitled, "The Emancipated Spectator." Here Rancière argued that in order to theatre to achieve its real essence, the spectator must be liberated from the traditional role of passive observer, must be "drawn into the magical power of theatrical action."[13] Although the terms *participatory* and *interactive* have often been applied to Punch-drunk and similar "immersive" productions, these are misleading. Although audience members share the same spaces and the same physical objects as the performers, they are not in fact encouraged to interact with them or in fact participate in the official "action" of the evening. A number of subsequent immersive productions have attempted to offer more actual participation. *Speakeasy Dollhouse*, which opened only a few months after *Sleep No More* and is also still running, is set in a 1920s bar. Audience members are encouraged to come in 1920s costumes, are assigned at the door "characters" in the play, and encouraged to interact (in character) with anyone they encounter. Once the specific "action" of the play, a murder and its consequences, begins, however, no audience member has the ability to interfere with or alter that action.

A certain degree of reality is necessary to the effect of such productions, but this reality is very carefully controlled. The environments are normally composed of real elements that the audience can manipulate, but these elements are carefully selected and placed. The real body of the actor can, to some degree, physically and verbally interact with the real body of the performer, but this activity also is totally circumscribed within the overall structure of the event. The closest model to such experiences is not actual life, as it is for Rancière, but rather virtual video games, in which one's character is free to move and make choices, but only within the parameters set forth by the game. One may see this influence clearly in the website of Punchdrunk, based on an interactive digital game. The spectator is in a sense emancipated, but it is in fact what might be called virtual emancipation. The spectator has changed from an observer to a player, but the game still remains some else's.

This largely illusory emancipation has important implications both for the theatre as an art form and as a social process. The enormous financial success of *Sleep No More*, the increasingly obvious commercialization of it and of many of its imitators, suggesting in many aspects the commercialization of theatrical experience by the Disney corporation, calls attention to another social structure whose ability and drive to consume everything it encounters exceeds even that of theatre, and that is the operations of capitalism. Just as modern theatre has at times almost obsessively consumed the surrounding real world, the operations of capitalism have sought to overtake this consumption by consuming this theatrical process, seeking to market and sell the "real" experience as a product.

This approach to immersive theatre has a very close connection to the widespread activity in contemporary culture to which Scott Magelssen, in the first major study of this phenomenon, has given the name *simming*, taken, he notes, from the vocabulary of on-line gaming. In the simming events Magelssen studies, "spectator-participants engage in the intentionally simulated production of some aspect of real or imagined society." They "try out an experience in situ, whether to practice for experiencing it in 'real life' or to bear witness to the experiences of those who have." He mentions as examples an ecopark in Mexico in which participants can pretend to be illegal immigrants crossing the border into the United States, and a historical museum in Indiana, where participants can pretend to be slaves on the Underground Railroad.[14]

Clearly activities of this sort are phenomenologically very close to so-called immersive theatre productions like *Speakeasy Dollhouse*, although at least so far the two activities see themselves and are seen apparently by those who participate in them, and by critics like Magelssen, as distinct activities. Experientially, though, there is clearly a great deal of overlap, especially in terms of the utilization of the real, which in both cases is primarily involved with the interaction of real bodies and real locations and physical objects. Perhaps the most important difference, at least in the sort of activities Magelssen considers, is that they are not generally narrative driven, but seek rather to capture a particular experience—such as a border crossing or a stopover on the Underground Railroad, seeking, at least in theory, to generate a "real" physical experience by mimetic means. In this, simmings reveal a close relationship to another popular form of imitative play, historical reenactments, where many participants seek to attain what the call a "period rush," during which mimesis disappears and their body actually experiences the enacted historical moment.[15]

So-called immersive theatre occupies a kind of middle-ground, placing the actual bodies of spectators into nontheatrical but still admittedly fictive worlds. The degree to which the spectators can interact with these worlds varies considerably. The work of Signa, a Copenhagen-based company formed in 2001, is similar in many respects to that of Punchdrunk but at least in some of its production allows the audience much more ability to alter the action.

Their *Ruby Town Oracle*, presented in several locations in Germany in 2008, offered a complete village of twenty-two buildings, presumably a political enclave that required a passport and visa to enter. It ran continuously for a week, during which time audiences could visit at any hour and for any length of time and encouraged free interaction with the more than forty "inhabitants." In other productions, beginning with the three "Twin Lives" plays with which Signa started, audience members have been encouraged not only to interact actively with the performers, but to create characters and plot developments on their own, to which the performers adapt. In these latter productions we seem to be close to Rancière's actively participating emancipated spectator. Yet, despite the radical phenomenological shift in the reception process, I argue that this emancipation is still, to a significant extent, illusory. In each of these productions the imaginary world, its locale, its properties, its rules, and its backstory remain the product of the creators. The spectators enter it as guests with their participation and knowledge always to a certain extent restricted by the "rules" of the experience, and its given circumstances.

Even with these restrictions, there is no question that during the past half-century, and particularly since the year 2000, the living body of the spectator has been welcomed into the fictive world of the theatre to an unprecedented extent and in a wide variety of ways. Having successfully absorbed and theatricalized the living body of the actor, the words and language of the surrounding culture, and the material objects of the "real" world, it would seem that what States called the theatre's appetite for the consumption of the real would have at last reached its limits, but within the wide variety of activities found in the world of immersive theatre, simmings, and reenactments can be found samples of this appetite extending even further and at last reaching outside the theatre to assimilate the grounds of the real itself, the experienced external world.

Given the infinite variety of that experience, it is hardly surprising that this latest expansion of the theatrical appetite has been stunningly varied in its manifestations and its relationship to the long history of representation and of theatre's relationship to the real. Despite the enormous variety found in simmings and immersive theatre and the widely varying degrees of freedom of interaction given to the audience within both of these now very popular forms, almost without exception these approaches still retain a fundamental organizational schema that has characterized the art of the theatre from the beginning. Most commonly, this schema has been manifested in the interaction of three components: the audience, the actors, and the "rules" of the event. The latter are normally a blend of general rules of the performance culture and the specific codes and rules of a particular event. These rules are understood by and sometimes created by the actors, and must be accepted by the audience as part of the unspoken contact that allows the performance to take place. The long-standing rule that actors and audiences inhabit separated spaces normally has been put aside in simmings and immersive theatre, but even though actors and audiences occupy the same space, and may indeed interact, they continue to inhabit separate mental worlds, one real and one fictive. Even in a production like *The Ruby Town Oracle*, where audience members may create new actions involving other audience members or townspeople, the townspeople remain psychically on the other side of a fictive line, playing "characters" that are not themselves and audience members predictably view their interventions as a kind of mimetic game, not really the same as the kind of interactions they might experience outside this fictive world.

The tradition of found objects and ready-mades in the world of art, however, have suggested a way to diminish this tie to the fictive world, or at least to place its functioning more directly under the control of the spectator. In a contemporary museum, few spectators would be surprised to encounter, for example, a real mop and bucket, which they are encouraged by the context and the tradition of "ready-mades" to consider as a work of art, not something left behind by a careless custodian, as would have certainly been the case in previous eras.

The phenomenologist Bruce Wilshire discusses a particularly theatrical version of this process in relation to a striking artistic experiment, *Light Touch*, created in 1976 by the New York visual artist Robert Whitman. Whitman created something very close to a traditional theatrical atmosphere by seating his audience as in a theatre but inside a trucking warehouse facing the main warehouse door, which was covered by curtains like a stage opening with a projected image on it. These curtains were then opened to reveal the actual street outside, like a stage setting. According to Wilshire, the normally banal spectacle of passing traffic was in this manner converted into a strange and fascinating kind of theatre simply by an alteration of perception:

> Cars appeared occasionally, framed by the door, as they passed on the street directly outside. Appeared, but appeared transfigured, as if a spell had been cast over them. Details of their shape and movement ordinarily not noticed, leapt out, as if from a numinous aura. It was as if cars were being seen for the first time.[16]

A more recent example of such experimentation, with a moving audience, was the 2009 production *The Provenance of Beauty*, created by the Foundry Theatre of New York, which has specialized in site-specific work. The performance was essentially a guided bus tour of the South Bronx, a part of New York rarely visited by tourists, the symbol of urban decay in the 1970s but since given new life by urban renewal and a strong alternative art scene, closely associated with such urban expressions as rap, hip-hop, and graffiti art. As the bus toured this complex, layered, and rapidly changing district, the "guide" pointed out places and even passing individuals as part of a poetic narrative. As with much promenade performance, the distinction between "real" and "staged" elements of the passing scene was deliberately left unclear and thus everything framed by the bus tour became part of the passing show.

The dynamics of increasingly common experiments of this sort were explored by semiotician Umberto Eco in one of the first essays on semiotics of the theatre, in 1977. Eco comments on a situation imagined by pioneer semiotician Charles Peirce wherein a drunken man is exposed in a public space by the Salvation Army in order to serve as a sign communicating a message about the negative effects of drink. What fascinated Eco about this situation was that the communication was not consciously produced by the drunken man but by an external agent, here the Salvation Army, that framed him in such a way that potential viewers, the audience, would see him as communicating a message. One might call this process "framing," following sociologist Erving Goffman, but Eco proposes instead the term *ostention*, a term from medieval logic, describing a situation where something is picked up among existing objects and consciously put on display for contemplation.[17] Clearly this process is involved in the art tradition of the found object as well as in theatrical experiments like *Light Touch* or *The Provenance of Beauty*.

Although the "scene" witnessed by the "audiences" of both these productions strikingly opened the "real" to imaginative theatricalization by those audiences, the physical relation between the viewer and the viewed remained quite traditional. Indeed, that helped encourage the operations of theatricalization, just as placing a mop and bucket on display in a museum encourages an "artistic" view of them. Inevitably, however, the interest during the past several decades in allowing the world of the spectator and that of the scene to interpenetrate led to works in which audiences, as it were, moved out into the street of *Light Touch* or got off of the Foundry Theatre tour bus and actually interacted with the people and objects placed on display. In short, they were encouraged to view the "real" world in which they were moving and with which they were directly interacting as an ostended spectacle.

To suggest the change from the promenade productions of the 1980s, to experiments of this kind around the turn of the century, we might look at a pivotal production by one of the leading theatrical experimental artists at the end of the last century, Reza Abdoh. Although all of Abdoh's productions utilized space and engaged and challenged audiences in strikingly unconventional ways, none expanded both of these areas so memorably as his first production in New York, *Father was a Peculiar Man*, in 1990. Not surprisingly, this production was created under the auspices of En Garde Arts, the leading site-specific theatre company in New York at that time. *Father Was a Peculiar Man*, based on Fyodor Dostoevsky's *Brothers Karamazov*, was staged in a several-square-block area of New York's Meatpacking district, a rather grim and forbidding area whose narrow, cobbled streets still somewhat suggest a nineteenth-century European city. Audiences were partly guided but for the most part free to wander through this area, where they witnessed some clearly staged scenes, but also many parts of the streetscape that may or may not be part of the production. Although the evening was quieter than the day, the life of the city continued. Clearly the dark blue limousine displaying American flags and John and Jacqueline Kennedy look-alikes in the rear was part of the show, but what about the line of cars and taxis following? Were they a cortege or just backed-up traffic? And what about people looking out of windows, or passed in the street. Were they actors, fellow spectators, or just citizens going about their own business? A calculated ambiguity between fictive and real characterized much of the event, and required audiences not only physically decide upon their trajectory through the area but mentally decide whether to consider the phenomena they were witnessing as a part of the real or the fictive world, or indeed to leave this question in a state of suspension.

Such an ambiguous interpenetration of real and fictive worlds moved from an obscure corner of Manhattan to its very heart, and from off-off Broadway to New York's theatrical center in 2003 with *The Angel Project*, created by Deborah Warner, one of England's best-known directors. *The Angel Project* began as a fairly typical 1995 promenade production, in which audience members were guided through a huge abandoned nineteenth-century London hotel, and urged to feel the presence of its ghosts. In 1999 Warner reconceived the piece as a walk through a cityscape, with the ghosts replaced by angels, watching over the city. This version was taken to Perth, Australia, in 2000 and to New York in 2003. In New York, the experience started in a part of the city even more remote and obscure than the Meatpacking district utilized by Abdoh. This was in a park at the end of Roosevelt Island, a small strip of land in New York's East River. Instructions given to participants sent them next by public transportation to Times Square, the central Manhattan district where most of the other eight stops were located, stops that ranged from an abandoned pornographic theatre to the elegant upper floors of the Chrysler Building. The mixture of real life and staged performance so clear in *Father Was a Peculiar Man* was much in evidence here also. As one reviewer observed:

> Walking around the city as part of the project opens up the possibility that anyone on the street might be an "angel." How about the homeless man in front of the Peep-o-rama, with his "Tell Me Off for $2" sign? Or the well-scrubbed teens in matching red "Bear His Name" t-shirts who swarm out of the 42 St. subway station? Warner leaves everything open, which helps you see the familiar with new eyes." [18]

There is a clear line of influence from the sort of production Abdoh offered in 1990, through the highly publicized *Angel Project* of British director Deborah Warner to the work of Punchdrunk, whose artistic director Felix Barrett has cited Warner's project as an important inspiration for his own work.[19]

Some of the leading contemporary experimental companies have explored variations of these ambiguous interweavings of theatrical and real elements. One might cite, for example, much of the work of Rimini Protokoll, founded in Berlin in 1999, whose aesthetic is essentially involved with the tension between the real and the theatrical. Probably their best known production internationally was the 2005 *Call Cutta*. In its original form, the production asked audience members to report to the Hebbel Theatre, a center for experimental work in Berlin, where they were given a mobile phone and connected with an operator in a call-center tower in another major city, but one on the opposite side of the globe, in Calcutta, India. The Indian operator then gave directions to the audience member, taking him or her on an individual, rambling tour through a generally unfamiliar and somewhat desolate section of the nearby Kreuzberg district. The production operated on a variety of experiential levels. In addition to being a kind of guided walking tour of an unusual Berlin neighborhood, it also involves a key period of Berlin history, since part of the trajectory touches on sites connected with German/Indian relations during the Nazi era. Moreover, the operator consciously attempted to build a personal, even romantic relationship with the spectator, adding another performative level to the experience. When I took this tour in the early summer of 2005 it had already been running for several weeks, and for part of the way I was followed by amused crowds of Turkish immigrant children who had obviously become accustomed to odd individuals like myself wandering abstractedly through their neighborhood following directions on headphones. For them, we and our guiding Indian spirits had also become an entertaining performance, part of the ongoing complex performance structure of the city itself.

During the second decade of the twenty-first century, Rimini Protokoll became a worldwide performance phenomenon and it is both striking and appropriate that its encouragement of its audiences to blend the real and the mimetic into playfully negotiated experience with different levels of reality and representation precisely reflects an important part of current discourse in the real represented, as I noted in the introduction, by such theorists as Liz Tomlin, Patrick Duggan, and Cormac Power. Articulations of contemporary shifting experiences of reality and representation such as Power's idea of levels of reality at play or Duggan's "mimetic shimmering," provide both a helpful vocabulary and a guide to the understanding of the strategies of work of this type.

Rimini Protokoll's ongoing *Remote* series clearly illustrates both the performance dynamics of such productions and also their current international significance. A group of around fifty participants assembles in an urban location and are issued radio headphones, within which a synthetic voice guides them through a series of city locations—a churchyard, city streets, gymnasia, public transport—providing a running commentary that encourages them to see the city and its activity as ostended, or theatricalized. Clearly this can be seen as a modern, much more sophisticated version of Whitman's experimental *Light Touch*—indeed, one sequence near the beginning of each *Remote* production is so similar to Whitman as to seem almost a conscious quotation of him. The ambulatory, head-set wearing participants are instructed by their invisible guide to stop within a cemetery but near the entrance and to observe the automobiles and pedestrians passing by outside the entry gate as if they were a part of a theatre piece.

The first articulation of this event experience was *Remote Berlin*, which took place in that city in the spring of 2013, starting at the Hebbel Theatre, which is Rimini Protokoll's home base. It was soon followed by *Remote Lisbon, Remote Hannover,* and *Remote Avignon,* built around similar walking tours in each of those cities. Before the end of 2013, Zurich, Basel, Vienna, and São Paulo had been added to the list. The global reach of the event continued to accelerate, with performances in 2014 in Bangalore, Lausanne, St. Petersburg, Vilnius, Milan, Le Havre, and Tallinn, and by the spring of 2013, two years after its first manifestation, in New York, Santiago, Antwerp, and Moscow.

Here again can be seen the convergence I mentioned earlier between modern theatre's consumption of reality and modern global capitalism's consumption of human activity of all sorts, including theatre. As modern performance has discovered the attraction to audiences of marketing the real and real experiences, or even of experiences of "mimetic shimmering," which have their own particular fascination, modern marketing has immediately seized upon this attraction, well aware that experience was a product as potentially commercial as any tangible good. The entire "immersive theatre" vogue, including the commercial use of that name, has clearly reflected this dynamic, not least in the burgeoning marketing of *Sleep No More*, the first major international success of this phenomenon. The continuing spread of *Remote* events across the globe provides an excellent example of another all-too-familiar operation of modern capitalism, the markets of international brands through widespread franchises, with experience now being the circulated project instead of hamburgers, coffee, or soft drinks.

With theatre's absorption of reality being in turn absorbed by the capitalist drive, performance seems to move ever more deeply into the domain of the simulacrum and repetition, and ever further from even the illusion of an unmediated reality to which theatre could hold up its mirror. Today that mirror is for the most part shattered, or held up against another mirror to create infinite reflections lacking any ultimate grounding. In even the most extreme, or the most commercialized of such contemporary performance activities, however, the operations of mimesis have not disappeared. One might expect that with a growing cultural assumption of the proposition that the world around us is composed of simulacra, of an infinite series of representations unsupported by a confirmable grounding, would result in a more neutral view of the world, in that the long-felt tension between the "real" and the imitation would no longer exist. By extension, the collapse of this binary would suggest a similar collapse of the appeal of theatre, which from its beginning has taken the tension of this binary as central to its experience and effect.

In fact, it is already clear that neither the growing dominance of the society of spectacle nor the growing commercialism of experience, which clearly reinforces the disappearance of what used to be seen as real into various forms of simulated reality has in fact diminished an interest in the kinds of performance created by these forces. What the increasing extension of the mimetic into the rest of the world clearly indicates that even as it apparently absorbs more and more of the traditional "real," it does not, within the realm of performative activity, remove the desire for and pleasure in the ongoing tension between belief and disbelief that has always been central to the theatre experience. The indeterminacy noted by Lehmann does not apparently result in indifference to the mimetic tension, but rather in recognition of the ability of the mind and body to play with this indeterminacy, to experiment with varieties and levels of the "real." Mimesis has not disappeared, but is now challenged by a contemporary extension of it into "mimetic shimmering." Through strategies such as these, modern theatre and performance continues their age-old role of serving as strategies to aide in the enrichment and understanding of the complexity of the human experience. Even if the real, to return to States's metaphor, has in the postmodern era been totally consumed, the nourishment provided by that consumption continues to provide ample energy for the continued relevance and importance of theatre and performance.

Notes

Introduction

1. *Physics* II 8.199a, 10–18.
2. Plato, *The Republic*, X, trans. Harold Bloom (New York: Basic Books, 1968), 279–80.
3. Ibid., 279.
4. Louis de Jaucourt, "Belle Nature," in *Encyclopedie methodique, ou par ordre des matières*, ed. Diderot and d'Alembert, 197 v. (Paris, 1782–1832), 11: 42.
5. Plotinus, *The Enneads*, trans. Stephen MacKenna (London: Lorenz Books, 1917–1930), V, 8, 1, 413
6. Aristotle, *Poetics*, trans. W. H. Butcher (University Park: University of Pennsylvania Press, 2000), I;3. 6.
7. Ibid., 6:12, 13.
8. Luigi Riccoboni, *Réflexions histoiques et critiques sur les différents théâtres de l'Europe* (Paris, 1738), 34.
9. Antonio Francesco Riccoboni, *L'Art du théâtre à Madame xxx* (Paris, 1750), 75.
10. Arthur Murphy, *The Life of David Garrick, Esq.* (Dublin, 1801), 21 (italics in original).
11. Victor Hugo, *Oeuvres complètes* 18 v. (Paris: Club français du livre, 1967), 3: 63–65.
12. Herbert F. Collins, *Talma: The Biography of an Actor* (New York: Hill & Wang, 1964), 322.
13. Emile Zola, *Oeuvres complètes*, 50 vols. (Paris: F. Bernard, 1927–29), 42:120.
14. David Belasco, *The Theatre Through Its Stage Door* (New York: Harper & Brothers, 1919), 76–77.
15. Keir Elam, *The Semiotics of Theatre and Drama* (London: Methuen, 1980), 23.
16. Peter Handke, *Kaspar and Other Plays*, trans. Michael Roloff (New York: Farrar, Straus and Giroux, 1969), 10–11.
17. Bert O. States, *Great Reckonings in Little Rooms* (Berkeley: University of California Press, 1985), 19–20.
18. Ibid., 40.
19. Ibid., 36.

20. Jean Jullien, *Le theatre vivant* (Paris; G. Charpentier, 1892), 11.

21. Alain Badiou, *The Century*, trans. Alberto Toscano (Cambridge: Polity, 2008), 50–56,

22. States. *Great Reckonings*, 40.

23. See, for example, Derrida's discussion of the sign in the first chapter of *Of Grammatology*, trans. Gayatri Spivak (Baltimore: Johns Hopkins University Press, 1997), 48–50.

24. Elinor Fuchs, "Presence and the Revenge of Writing: Re-thinking Theatre after Derrida," *Performing Arts Journal* 9, no. 2/3 (1985): 163–73, and *The Death of Character* (Bloomington: University of Indiana Press, 1996).

25. Hans-Thies Lehmann, *Postdramatic Theatre*, trans. Karen Jüers-Munby (London: Routledge, 2006). 37.

26. Liz Tomlin, *Acts and Apparitions: Discourses on the Real in Performance Practice and Theory, 1990–2010* (Manchester: Manchester University Press, 1913).

27. Patrick Duggan, *Trauma-Tragedy: Symptoms of Contemporary Performance* (Manchester: Manchester University Press, 2012).

28. Lehmann, *Postdramatic*, 134, quoted in Tomlin, *Acts*, 45.

29. Lehmann, *Postdramatic*, 100.

30. Andrew Quick, "approaching the real: reality effects and the play of fiction," *Performance Research* 1, no. 3 (1996): 16.

31. Stephen Bottoms, "Authorizing the Audience: The Conceptual Drama of Tim Crouch," *Performance Research* 14, no. 1 (2009): 74.

32. Tomlin, *Acts*, 75.

33. Cormac Power, *Presence in Play: A Critique of Theories of Presence in the Theatre* (Amsterdam and New York: Rodopi, 2008), 9.

Chapter 1

1. Bert O. States, *Great Reckonings in Little Rooms* (Berkeley: University of California Press, 1985), 27.

2. Viktor Shklovsky, "Art as Technique," in *Russian Formalist Criticism: Four Essays*, trans. Lee T. Lemon and Marion J. Rees (Lincoln: University of Nebraska Press, 1965), 12, quoted in States, *Great Reckonings*, 21.

3. J. L. Austin, *How to Do Things with Words*, 22. Although this distinction was also maintained by John R. Searle, later theorists, headed by Derrida, have mounted serious challenges to it. I have summarized this debate in my book *Performance: A Critical Introduction* (London: Routledge, 1998), 60–66.

4. Sean Zwagerman, *Wit's End: Women's Humor as Rhetorical and Performative Strategy* (Philadelphia: University Pennsylvania Press, 2010), 26.

5. Such as Puck's famous exhortation to the audience at the end of *A*

Midsummer Night's Dream, "Give me your hands, if we be friends," clearly an invitation to applause, although Peter Brook ingeniously reinterpreted it, with his entire company reaching across the footlights to join hands with their public.

6. Not even necessarily words the audience understands, as in the opening of Sarah Ruhl's 2004 *The Clean House*, which consists of a lengthy joke given directly to the audience in Portuguese.

7. One might argue that the breakdown of language found in some of the works of Ionesco or Churchill provides a kind of parallel to the actor, for whatever reason, "breaking out of character" and thus opening a crack in the fiction through which reality can be seen, but I think that what these works are exploring is rather the constructedness and arbitrariness of language in general, both within the theatre and outside.

8. Erwin Piscator, "A Letter to the Weltbühne," rpt. In *World Theatre* 17 (1968): 329.

9. Attilio Favorini, "Introduction," in *Voicings: Ten Plays from the Documentary Theater* (Hopewell, NY: Ecco, 1995), xviii. I am much indebted to Favorini's excellent historical survey of this genre.

10. Piscator, "Letter," 329.

11. Hans-Thies Lehmann, *Postdramatisches Theater* (Frankfurt am Main: Verlag der Autoren, 1999).

12. Lynn Mally, "The Americanization of the Soviet Living Newspaper," *The Carl Beck Papers in Russian and East European Studies* 1903 (February 2008), 4.

13. See Natasha Kolchevska, "Toward a 'Hybrid' Literature: Theory and Praxis of the *Faktoviki*," *Slavic and East European Journal* 27, no. 4 (1983): 452–64.

14. Peter Weiss, "Fourteen Propositions for a Documentary Theatre," in Favorini, *Voicings*, 139.

15. Donald Freed "The Case and the Myth: *The United States of America v. Julius and Ethel Rosenberg*," in Favorini, *Voicings*, 202.

16. Ibid.

17. Dan Isaac, "Theatre of Fact," *The Drama Review: TDR* 15, no. 3 (Summer, 1971): 132.

18. See Hayden White, "Interpretation in History," *New Literary History* 4, no. 2 (Winter 1973): 281–314.

19. See Michael Vanden Heuvel, "L.S.D. (Let's Say Deconstruction!)," in *The Wooster Group and Its Traditions*, ed. Johan Callens (Brussels: Peter Lang, 2004), 71–82.

20. David Savran, *Breaking the Rules: The Wooster Group* (New York: Theatre Communications Group, 1986).

21. Ibid., 51–52.

22. Favorini, "Introduction," xxxvi.

23. David Pellegrini, "Unquestioned Integrity Questioned," in Favorini, *Voicings,* 374.

24. Beth Potier, "Mother of Documentary Theater Brings Her 'Children' to Loeb Drama Center," *Harvard University Gazette,* December 12, 2002.

25. Athol Fugard, "Introduction," in *Testimonies: Four Plays by Emily Mann* (New York: Theatre Communications Group, 1997), xiii.

26. Christopher Bigsby, *Contemporary American Playwrights* (New York: Cambridge University Press, 1999), 138.

27. David Savran, *In Their Own Words: Contemporary American Playwrights* (New York: Theatre Communications Group, 1988), 151.

28. Gary Fisher Dawson, *Documentary Theatre in the United States* (Westport, CT: Greenwood Press, 1999), 164.

29. Kathleen Betsko and Rachel Koenig, *Interviews with Contemporary Women Playwrights* (New York: Beech Tree Books, 1987), 275.

30. Studs Terkel, *Working: People Talk About What They Do All Day and How They Feel About What They Do* (New York: Pantheon Books, 1974).

31. Elin Schoen Brockman, "Ideas and Trends; for the Jaded Aesthete, A Dose of the Very Real," *New York Times,* May 16, 1999.

32. Jesse McKinley, "Play about Demonstrator's Death is Delayed," *New York Times,* February 28, 2006.

33. Terry Stoller, *Tales of the Tricycle Theatre* (London: Bloomsbury, 2013), 143–96.

34. Ibid., 162.

35. "Guantanamo," Tricycle Theatre website, www.tricycle.co.uk/home/about-the-tricycle-pages/about-us-tab-menu/archive/archived-theatre-production/guantanamo-honor-bound-to-defend-freedom/.

36. "But is it Theatre?" *Economist,* July 1, 2004. Online version: www.economist.com/node/2876778.

37. See Marvin Carlson, "Performing the Self," *Modern Drama* 39, no. 4 (1996): 699–806.

38. David Hare, "Why fabulate?" *The Guardian,* Feb. 1, 2002.

39. Neal Ascherson, "Whose Line is it Anyway?" *The Observer,* Nov. 9, 2004.

40. Quoted in Ascherson, "Whose Line."

41. Stephen Bottoms, "Putting the Document into Documentary: An Unwelcome Corrective?" *TDR* 50, no. 3 (Fall, 2006): 17.

42. *Village Voice,* April 21, 1980, 84.

43. Quoted in Spalding Gray, *The Journal of Spalding Gray,* ed. Nell Casey (New York: Vintage, 2011), 69.

44. "Nature Theater of Oklahoma," Foundation for Contemporary Arts website, http://www.foundationforcontemporaryarts.org/grant_recipients/nature-theater-of-4.html

45. Hilton Als, "Eight Hours of, Like, Life," *New Yorker,* January 23, 2013.

Chapter 2

1. See, for example, Mark Nielsen, "Imitation, Pretend Play, and Childhood: Essential Elements in the Evolution of Human Culture?" *Journal of Comparative Psychology* 126, no. 2 (May 2012): 170–81.

2. Richard Southern, *The Seven Ages of the Theatre* (New York: Hill & Wang, 1961), 29–30.

3. James Laver, *Drama: Its Costume and Décor* (London: Studio, 1961), 153.

4. Pat Easterling, "Actor as Icon," in *Greek and Roman Actors: Aspects of an Ancient Profession*, ed. Pat Easterling and Edith Hall (Cambridge: Cambridge University Press, 2002), 327–41.

5. *New Theatre Quarterly* 4, no. 22 (May,1990): 154–61.

6. See František Deák, "Structuralism in Theater: The Prague School Contribution," *Drama Review* 20, no. 4 (December 1976): 83–94.

7. Quinn, "Celebrity," 155.

8. Ibid., 156.

9. Ibid, 160.

10. Ibid.

11. Dan Sullivan, "Madonna Panned and Mamet Praised for 'Speed-the-Plow," *Los Angeles Times*, February 7, 1988.

12. Jean Alter, *A Sociosemiotic Theory of Theatre* (Philadelphia: University of Pennsylvania Press, 1990), 32.

13. Quoted in Marvin Carlson, *The Italian Shakespearians* (Cranbury, NJ: Associated University Presses, 1985), 31.

14. Robert A. Carter, *Buffalo Bill Cody: The Man Behind the Legend* (New York: John Wiley, 2000), 147. Eventually over 550 dime novels were written about Buffalo Bill by Buntline and many others. In researching this area I discovered that much of the material I found in Carter's book was almost a literal but unacknowledged rephrasing of material from Don Russell, *The Lives and Legends of Buffalo Bill* (Norman: University of Oklahoma Press, 1960).

15. William F. Cody, *An Autobiography of Buffalo Bill* (New York: Cosmopolitan Book Corporation 1920), 310

16. Don Russell, *The Wild West* (Fort Worth, TX: Amon Carter Museum, 1970), 26.

17. Gary C. Anderson, *Sitting Bull and the Paradox of Lakota Nationhood* (New York: Pearson Education, 2007), 86.

18. Russell, *The Wild West*, 62.

19. Quoted in Russell, 65.

20. In 1645, even while the English Civil War was still in progress, parliamentarian troops restaged one of their recent victories at Blackheath (Howard Giles, "A Brief History of Re-enactment"), www.eventplan.co.uk/page29html. Similarly, in 1792, only a week after the Battle of Jemappes,

conscripted actors in the French army who had just fought the battle performed in a ballet version of the battle on the same field. See Marvin Carlson, *The Theatre of the French Revolution* (Ithaca, NY: Cornell University Press, 1966), 138. In both cases, of course, actors played the enemy.

21. The *Wikipedia* entry on reenactments claims that the survivors of the 7th Cavalry reenacted the battle for photographers in 1877, a year later, but this is denied by the standard book on the subject, Debra Buchholtz's *The Battle of the Greasy Grass/Little Bighorn: Custer's Last Stand in Memory, History and Popular Culture* (New York: Routledge, 2012). According to Buchholtz, the first reenactment of the battle was in fact staged by the Crow Indians in 1891, a different tribe. However, in 1910, the Bureau of Indian Affairs staged a celebration called "The Last Great Indian Council" (which, despite the name, was repeated for several years thereafter) held on the actual site of the battle. Part of the celebrations was a battle reenactment, the first featuring Indians actually involved in the original fight (107).

22. Slavoj Žižek, "A Plea for Leninist Intolerance," *Critical Inquiry* 29, no. 2 (Winter 2002): 559–60.

23. The New York Neo-Futurists, founded in 2004, began their manifesto by advocating "the complete inclusion and awareness of the actual world within the theatre." www.nyneofurturists.org/about/.

24. See, for example, the extended defense of this endeavor by Doctor Hinkfuss given to the audience at the opening of *Tonight We Improvise* (New York: E.P. Dutton, 1932).

25. Allan Kaprow, *Assemblages, Environments, and Happenings* (New York: Harry N. Abrams, 1966), 188–92.

26. Marvin Carlson, *Performance: A Critical Introduction* (London: Routledge, 1998), 102.

27. Willoughby Sharp and Liza Bear, Interview with Chris Burden, *Avalanche* 8 (1973), 61.

28. Garrett G. Fagan, *The Lure of the Arena* (Cambridge: Cambridge University Press, 2011), 6.

29. Jody Enders, *Death by Drama and other Medieval Urban Legends* (Chicago: University of Chicago Press, 2005).

30. Herbert F. Collins, *Talma: The Biography of an Actor* (New York: Hill & Wang, 1964), 321. This is not strictly true. As early as 1792 in Ducis's neoclassical adaptation of *Othello*, with Talma in the title role, the heroine, Heldemone, was killed in her bed (by stabbing, not strangling) in the original version, but when the play was first staged at the Comédie Française, the audience was so outraged that Ducis created a new happy ending, requiring neither Heldemone's death nor her bed.

31. Collins, 322.

32. Andrew Friedman, "The Total Radical Fiction: Vegard Vinge and Ida Müller's Ibsen-Saga," *Theater* 42, no. 3 (2012): 20.

33. John H. Houchin, *Censorship of the American Theatre in the Twentieth Century* (New York: Cambridge University Press, 2003), 205.

34. Letter of Rainer to Debra Jowitt, quoted in Jowitt, "The Story of a Woman Who . . . ," *Village Voice*, April 12, 1973.

35. Quoted in Leo Rubinstein, "Through Western Eyes," *Art in America* 66, no. 5 (September–October 1978): 75.

36. David Román, *Acts of Intervention: Performance, Gay Culture and AIDS* (Bloomington: Indiana University Press, 1998), 142.

37. This quote is widely reproduced but never, so far as I have been able to discover, with full attribution. It appears to be a regular part of international publicity for the company. See, for example, the media release of the 2014 Perth International Festival in Australia, http://media2.perthfestival_Situation-Rooms_MRO7112013.pdf.

38. Hannah Pilarcyzk, "Is Volker Lösch Germany's Most Controversial Director?" *Guardian*, March 18, 2011.

39. Ibid.

Chapter 3

1. Bert O. States, *Great Reckonings in Little Rooms: On the Phenomenology of Theatre* (Berkeley: University of California Press, 1985), 46–47.

2. Keir Elam, *The Semiotics of Theatre and Drama* (London: Methuen, 1980), 22–23.

3. George Grove, *Grove's Dictionary of Music and Musicians*, 9 vols. (Oxford: Oxford University Press, 1954), V, 319.

4. Grace Frank, "Genesis and Staging of the *Jeu d'Adam*," *PMLA* 39 (1944): 7–17.

5. Jean Jacquot, *La vie théâtrale au temps de la Renaissance*, quoted in Elie Konigson, *L'espace théâtrale médiéval* (Paris: Centre National de la Recherche Scientifique, 1975), 95.

6. R.T.R. Clark, *Myth and Symbol in Ancient Egypt* (London: Thames and Hudson, 1959), 65.

7. *Egeria: Diary of a Pilgrimage*, trans. and ed. George E. Gingras (New York: Paulist Press, 1970), 103–5.

8. Elizabeth Barlow Rogers, *Landscape Design: A Cultural and Architectural History* (New York: Harry N. Abrams, 2001), 179.

9. Gisela Sichardt, *Das Weimarer Liebhabertheater unter Goethes Leitung* (Weimar: Arlon Verlag, 1957), 62–64.

10. Victor Hugo, *Oeuvres completes*, 18 vols. (Paris Club Français du livre, 1967–70), 3:62–63.

11. John William Cole, *Life and Theatrical Times of Charles Kean*, 2 vols. (London: R. Bentley), 2:366.

12. Jerome Alfred Hart, *Sardou and the Sardou Plays* (Philadelphia: Lippincott, 1913), 266.

13. From the *Examiner*, February 24, 1833, quoted in *Romantic and Revolutionary Theatre, 1789–1859*, eds. Donald Roy, Victor Emeljanow (Cambridge; Cambridge University Press, 2003), 243.

14. Orville K. Larsen, *Scene Design in the American Theatre from 1915 to 1960* (Fayetteville: University of Arkansas Press, 1989), 21–22.

15. Wendell Philipps, "Staging a Popular Restaurant," *Theatre Magazine*, October 1912, 104.

16. Quoted in Lise-Lone Marker, *David Belasco: Naturalism in the American Theatre* (Princeton, NJ: Princeton University Press, 1975), 66.

17. Quoted in Andres Wengrow, "Robert Redington Sharpe: A Designer Rediscovered," *Theatre Design and Technology* 27, no. 1 (Winter 1991): 22.

18. Anon., "A Pastoral Performance," *Era*, June 6, 1885, 12.

19. Anon., "The Pastorall Players, *Eastward Ho!*, May 1885, 429.

20. Anon., "The Sherborne Pageant 1905: The Mother of All Pageants," www.historicalpageants.ac.uk/pageant-month/sherborne-pageant-1905/.

21. See Peter Merrington, "Staging History, Inventing Heritage: the 'New Pageantry' and British Imperial Identity, 1905–1935," in *Archaeologies of the British*, ed. Susan Lawrence (London: Routledge, 2003), 239–58.

22. Anon., "London Lays Plans for Elaborate Pageant," January 22, 2010, 10.

23. J. L. Styan, *Max Reinhardt* (Cambridge: Cambridge University Press, 1982), 18.

24. Hugo von Hofmannsthal, "Reinhardt as an International Force," in *Max Reinhardt and His Theatre*, ed. Oliver M. Sayler (New York: Brentano's, 1924), 26–27.

25. *Daily Telegraph*, June 16, 1933, quoted in Styan, 59

26. Hofmannsthal, "Reinhardt," 25.

27. Gusti Adler, quoted in *Max Reinhardt, 1873–1973: A Centennial Festschrift*, eds. George Wellwarth and Alfred Brooks (Binghamton, NY, 1973), 20.

28. Erika Fischer-Lichte, "Theatre as Festival Play: Max Reinhardt's Production of *The Merchant of Venice*, in *Venetian Views, Venetian Blinds: English Fantasies of Venice*, eds. Manfred Pfister and Barbara Schaff (Amsterdam: Rodopi, 1999), 175–79.

29. *Daily Telegraph*, (June 4, 1937), *The Sphere* (June 12, 1937), quoted in Robert Shaughnessy, *The Shakespeare Effect: A History of Twentieth-Century Performance* (Houndmills: Palgrave, 2002), 108–9.

30. Ibid., 108.

31. Quoted, ibid.

32. Nikolai Evreinov, *Histoire du théâtre russe*, trans. G. Welter (Paris: Editions du Chêne, 1947), 146.

33. See www.festivals.com/viewevent.aspx?eventid=Iz7XjC6G%2BzU%3D.

34. Although created for this specific location, *Roof Piece* has since been revived at other locations, most notably on the fortieth anniversary of its creation on the roof of the Getty Center in Los Angeles in 2013.

35. IOU statement of policy, quoted in Alison Oddey, *Devising Theatre: A Practical and Theoretical Handbook* (New York: Routledge, 1994), 126.

36. Mike Pearson, *Gllimpses of the Map; Cardiff Laboratory Theatre 1974–1980* (Cardiff Laboratory Theatre, 1980), 32.

37. Pearson, *Site-Specific Performance* (Houndmills: Palgrave, 2010), 4.

38. Armand Gatti, "Armand Gatti on Time, Place, and the Theatrical Event," trans. Nancy Oakes, *Modern Drama* 25, no. 1 (March 1982): 71.

39. Ibid., 72.

40. And occasionally even inside a theatre. Mac Wellman's *Crowbar* was presented in 1990 in the then-abandoned Victory Theatre on 42 Street by En Garde Arts, the leading New York company presenting site-specific work in the 1990s. Today the building, as the New Victory, has been restored to its original theatrical function.

41. Marvin Carlson, *Performance: A Critical Introduction* (London: Routledge, 1996), 119.

42. Suzi Gablik, *The Reenchantment of Art* (London: Thames and Hudson, 1991), 77, 87–88.

43. Quoted in Gablik, *Reenchantment*, 88.

Chapter 4

1. In the first major theoretical study of stage properties, *The Stage Life of Props* (Ann Arbor: University of Michigan Press, 2003), Andrew Sofer distinguishes between props, which are actually used or manipulated by the actors, and stage objects, which are not. For his purposes, this is an important distinction, but I am considering a different aspect of this question, which concerns both equally, so I will draw examples from both.

2. Sofer, *Stage Life*, 24.

3. Complicite, *Plays: 1* (London: Methuen, 2003), 133.

4. For an excellent summary of the origins and subsequent history of this story, see Leofranc Holford-Strevens, "Polus and His Urn: A Case Study in the Theory of Acting, c. 300 B.C.-c. A.D. 2000," *International Journal of the Classical Tradition* 11, no. 4 (Spring 2005): 499–523.

5. Denis Diderot, *Paradox sur le comédien, Oeuvres complètes*, ed. Herbert Diekmann et al. (Paris: R. Laffont, 1995), 128.

6. Sofer, *Stage Life*, 108–9.

7. Dutton Cook, "Stage Properties," *Belgravia*, 35 (1878), 287–88.

8. George Vandenhoff, *Leaves from an Actor's Note-Book* (New York: Appleton, 1860), 100.

9. "Jefferson Miscellany," *Jeffline: Highlight of the University Archives*

and Special Collections, http://jeffline.jefferson.edu;SML/Archives/Highlights/Miscellany.

10. Robert S. Menchin, *Where there's a Will: A Collection of Wills— Hilarious, Incredible, Bizarre. Witty . . . Sad* (Lincoln, NE; iUniverse, 1979o), 48.

11. Daniel Traister, "The Furness Memorial Library," in *the Penn Library Collections at 250: From Franklin to the Web* (Philadelphia: University of Pennsylvania Library, 2000), 76.

12. Percy Hetherington Fitzgerald, *Henry Irving: A Record of Twenty Years at the Lyceum* (London: Chapman and Hall, 1893), 313.

13. *Peter Hall's Diaries: The Story of a Dramatic Battle*, ed. John Goodwin (London, 1983), 195.

14. Quoted in Pascal Aebischer, *Shakespeare's Violated Bodies: Stage and Screen Performance* (Cambridge: Cambridge University Press, 2004), 86.

15. Ted Friend, "Skullduggery," *New Yorker*, October 9, 2006, 29–30.

16. Miriam Bratu Hansen, "Benjamin's Aura," *Critical Inquiry* 34 (Winter 2008): 340.

17. This is not entirely an aesthetic matter. According to union regulations, costumes and properties from commercial theatres in the United States cannot be reused in another professional production, although they can be stored and exhibited in museums and special collections.

18. Quoted in Sherifa Zuhur, ed., *Colors of Enchantment: Theater, Dance, Music, and the Visual Arts of the Middle East.* (Cairo: American University Press, 2003), 83.

19. Tate Wilkinson, *Memoirs*, 4 vols. (York: Wilson, Spence and Mawman, 1790), 4:92.

20. Eduard Genast, *Aus dem Tagebuch eines alten Schauspielers* (Leipzig, 1862), 1:141.

21. Vladimir Nemorovich-Danchenko, *My Life in the Russian Theatre*, trans. John Cournos (New York: Little, Brown, 1936), 90.

22. Tadeusz Kantor, "The Impossible Theatre 1969–73," in *A Journey Through Other Spaces: Essays and Manifestos, 1944–1990*, ed. and trans. by Michal Kobialka (Berkeley: University of California Press, 1993), 90, 118.

23. David Savran, *Breaking the Rules: The Wooster Group* (New York: Theatre Communications Group, 1986), 51–52.

24. Théodore Child, "Othello in Paris," *Poet-Lore* 1 (1889): 306.

25. Dennis Bartholomeusz, *The Winter's Tale in Performance in England and America 1811–1976*, (London: Cambridge University Press, 2011), 97.

26. *Western Daily Press*, October 11, 1864, quoted in John Stokes, *Resistible Theatres* (New York: Barnes and Noble, 1972), 37.

27. In Ferdinand Icre's 1888 *The Butchers*.

28. Erin Rebecca Bone Steele, "Murder and Melodramatic Borrowings," *Theatre Symposium* 19 (2011): 17.

29. Robert A. Carter, *Buffalo Bill Cody: The Man Behind the Legend* (New York: John Wiley, 2000), 247.

30. *Chicago Sunday Tribune*, January 13, 1889.

31. Detailed descriptions of performances by lions, elephants, goats, cats, dogs, bears, and monkeys are included in *The Amazing Preacher and the Stranger*, a play written in Cairo in the late thirteenth century by Ibn Daniual. *Theatre from Medieval Cairo*, ed. Safi Mahfouz and Marvin Carlson (New York: Martin E. Segal Theatre Center, 2013), 121–33.

32. Shakespeare, *Henry V*, Prologue.

33. Bert O. States, *Great Reckonings in Little Rooms* (Berkeley, University of California Press, 1985), 33.

34. Jim Bondeson, *Amazing Dogs: A Cabinet of Canine Curiosities* (The Hill, Stroud: Amberly Publishing, 2011), section 5 (unpaginated).

35. Samuel Pepys, *The Diary of Samuel Pepys* (London: Macmillan, 1905), 666.

36. Claude and François Parfaict, *Histoire du théâtre François*, 15 vols. (Paris, 1745–49), 12:230.

37. Théophile Gautier, *Histoire de l'art dramatique en France depuis vingt-cinq ans* (Paris: Editions Hetzel, 1859), 4:210.

38. Marian Hanna Winter, *The Theatre of Marvels* (New York: Benjamin Blom, 1962), 187.

39. Gautier, *Histoire*, 1:337.

40. Charles Dibden, *The Professional Life of Mr. Dibdin, Written by Himself*, 4 vols. (London, 1803), 2:105.

41. Bondeson, *Amazing Dogs*, section 5 (unpaginated).

42. Gary Jay Williams, *Our Moonlight Revels: A Midsummer Night's Dream in the Theatre* (Iowa City: University of Iowa Press, 1997), 141.

43. Quoted in Hilary de Vries, "A Really Big Show," *Los Angeles Times*, September 20, 1990.

44. Ben Brantley, "Plotting the Grid of Sensory Overload," *New York Times*, October 6, 2014.

Chapter 5

1. Eric Bentley, *The Life of the Drama* (New York: Atheneum, 1964), 150.

2. Ibid., 40.

3. Lawrence Rainey, Christine Poggi, and Laura Wittman, eds. *Futurism : An Anthology* (New Haven, CT: Yale University Press, 2009), 163.

4. An excellent example is the series of Ibsen adaptations created in Norway and England between 2009 and 2014 by Vegard Vinge and Ida Müller, whose audiences are subjected to assaults going far beyond Marinetti's suggestions. See Andrew Friedman, "The Total Radical Fiction," *Theater Magazine* 42, no. 3 (2012): 11–29.

5. Jean-Jacques Rousseau, *Oeuvres*, 25 vols. (Paris, 1823–26), 2:24–26.

6. Augusto Boal, *Theatre of the Oppressed*, trans. C. A. and M.-O. L. McBride (New York: Urizen, 1979), 139.

7. Richard Schechner, *Environmental Theater* (New York: Hawthorne Books, 1973), 45. The chapter "Participation" appears on pages 40–86.

8. Ibid.

9. Allan Kaprow, *Assemblages, Environments, and Happenings* (1966), 168, quoted in Schechner, *Environmental*, 61.

10. "Words from Ian McKellen," 2003, www.mckellen.com/stage/coriolanus.

11. Brooks McNamara, Jerry Rojo, and Richard Schechner, *Theatres, Spaces, Environments* (New York: Drama Publishers, 1975), 32.

12. Leslie Bennetts, "Staging 'La Strada' in a Vermont Field Requires Invention," *New York Times*, July 21, 1987.

13. Jacques Rancière, "The Emancipated Spectator," *Art Forum*, March 2007, 272.

14. Scott Magelssen, *Simming: Participatory Performance and the Making of Meaning* (Ann Arbor: University of Michigan Press 2014), 5.

15. Rebecca Schneider, *Performing Remains: Art and War in Times of Theatrical Reenactment* (New York: Routledge, 2011), 41.

16. Bruce Wilshire, *Role Playing and Identity* (Bloomington: Indiana University Press, 1982), x.

17. Umberto Eco, "The Semiotics of Theatrical Performance," *TDR* 21 (1977): 112.

18. www.Criticbigot.com, posted November 16, 2010.

19. Quoted in Hermione Eyre, "How Punchdrunk Theatre Troup is Taking over the World, *London Evening Standard*, September 2, 2011, www.standard.co.uk/lifestyle/esmagazine/how-punchdrunk-theatre-troup-is-taking-over-the-world-6439363.html.

Index